How To Lose A
Highlander

The MacGregor Lairds

How To Lose A
Highlander

The MacGregor Lairds

Michelle
McLean

Entangled Publishing, LLC
2614 South Timberline Road
Suite 109
Fort Collins, CO 80525
Visit our website at www.entangledpublishing.com.

Scandalous is an imprint of Entangled Publishing, LLC.

Edited by Erin Molta
Cover design by Erin Dameron-Hill
Cover art from Shutterstock

Manufactured in the United States of America

First Edition June 2017

SCANDALOUS

Hey Mom—Good news, you can read this one!

Chapter One

Sorcha Campbell hurried down the corridor toward the music hall, the ringlets gathered by her ears bouncing madly in her haste. She was late again. Her father would scold her for certain. The faint sounds of laughter and tuning instruments made her quicken her pace. King Charles II himself would be attending tonight's masquerade ball, and Sorcha was supposed to be making a good impression.

Her father had been summoned to the Palace of Whitehall in London a fortnight ago in response to his petition for aid against the MacGregors. That clan had been a thorn in the side of the Campbells for centuries. But lately the raids had been intolerable. And it seemed as though the king would finally listen to her father's complaints, in particular against the nearest neighbor to her father's estates, Malcolm MacGregor, Laird of Glenlyon.

While her father was certain the king would side with the Campbells, he had still wished for Sorcha to be present to aid in whatever way possible. In other words, to draw the king's eye and hopefully, his favor. Charles liked pretty and vivacious women. Sorcha didn't care for being paraded about like some strumpet. However, if a few well-timed smiles could help her family, it was a small enough thing to ask. As long as that was all her father expected of her. She wouldn't play the whore. Not even to the king to help her family.

But she supposed a little flirting was harmless enough. She'd lived at court with her mother and then her mother's kin her whole life, except for those horrible years when Oliver Cromwell, the so-called Lord Protector, had ruled. However, since Charles Stewart had regained his throne, she hadn't been much in the king's presence. Which meant she'd be fresh enough to distract him.

Sorcha turned the corner and ran straight into the solid wall of someone's chest.

"Oh!" she said, nearly falling backward.

A hand reached out and grabbed her arm before she went down. "My apologies, lass. I didna see you there."

"It's all right, no harm was done," she said, more concerned that her ornate costume had sustained no damage. She patted her headdress, assuring that the jeweled and gold filigree peacock head mask was still in place, its matching plumage still gathered becomingly at her crown.

She glanced up into the amused eyes of a huge brute of a man dressed in a rich coat and vest, a pleated kilt in place of the usual silk breeches. Her eyes widened at his bare knees and muscular calves and she couldn't help but wonder what was hidden by the draped cloth of his kilt. More of the same hardened muscles as the rest of him, she was sure. His face was almost entirely covered by an elaborate mask that resembled the gaping open mouth of a lion. Only his eyes, lips, and chin were visible. And his eyes...the color of warm amber that gave his mask a haunting realness that made her step back.

Judging by his speech and dress, the man was a Scot. And a warrior from the look of him. She'd spent so much time at court of late she'd grown used to the softer courtiers who frequented the palace, rather than the sturdy, battle-hardened men of the country of her birth. Perhaps she should have insisted upon more visits to her father's lands in Scotland. She'd never had any real desire to do so in the past and hadn't strayed far past Edinburgh when her father did insist upon her presence.

She liked living at court. It was like living in a city within a city, always surrounded by throngs of people from every walk of life; from the servants who waited on them to the nobles she'd grown up with, to the foreign diplomats with their exotic eccentricities. Where else would she be able to walk the halls and meet such an array of exciting people? Just the other day she'd run into an outlandish noble from the Orient; the court's master painter from Holland who had just finishing a portrait of the queen and was on his way to paint the king's chief mistress; and a courtier who had recently returned from France, overflowing with ideas on new fashions.

Court life was exhilarating and surreal. She enjoyed the balls, and parties, fancy gowns and gaiety that abounded, especially since the king's return. But, for the first time, she realized she might have been hasty in her assumption that there was nothing worth missing in Scotland.

She dredged up her most brilliant smile and took care to look the man right in the eyes.

"I believe I'm the one who owes you an apology, sir. I'm afraid I was in a hurry and wasn't watching where I was going."

"Apology accepted," he said, bending over her hand to place a kiss on its back.

Those eyes watched hers, as if he waited for her to yank her hand from his. She stood steady while he kissed her hand, her mouth opening a bit to suck in a breath of air when his lips lingered. If he expected her to flutter her fan and swoon at his feet, he'd be sorely disappointed. She was a Campbell. A slightly out of place one, but she still had her father's fiery blood running through her veins. She had no fear of anything, and certainly not of a man who was taking more liberties with his courtly greeting than he should. She'd been the focus of far more brazen attentions. Though never from anyone half so appealing.

Two ladies sauntered by, and Sorcha noted with interest that they took care to give the gentleman a wide berth.

"I'm afraid some of the ladies here at court dinna find me much to their liking. Perhaps I offend their sensibilities," he said, releasing her hand.

Sorcha waved them off. "Silly fools, the lot of them. Most of them find anyone from farther north than York terrifying. My mother was English and spent most of her life here, and I have scarce traveled from court, except during those dreadful years when our king was in exile. And for someone of your... imposing stature," she said, looking him over from the top of the deep red, unpowdered, and unwigged hair flowing out from behind the mask, to the tip of the boots he wore, instead of the small heels favored by most of the men at court, "well, perhaps your presence merely overwhelms them."

The man laughed softly, the low rumbling sound emanating from his chest like the purr of a cat. "Aye, I suppose. Though it doesna seem to have that effect on you," he said, giving her an appraising look of his own.

She smiled. "I was born in Scotland and have spent a fair amount of time around men such as you."

"Is that so?" His eyes widened behind the mask, and the blush she'd been trying to contain stole into her cheeks.

"Well, perhaps not quite like you."

"And I've never had the pleasure of meeting a lady quite so lovely," he said, his gaze roaming over her.

She tried to keep her composure, though a man looking upon her with such obvious appreciation was an experience she enjoyed more than she expected. Oh, he was not the first man to gaze at her with lustful intentions. She'd certainly had her fair share of lecherous looks. But the quiet smolder burning in his eyes sent a tingle through her body, unlike anything she'd ever felt before.

Strains of music floated down the hall to them and Sorcha gasped. "I must go!"

"May I escort ye to the ball, my beautiful peacock?"

Sorcha hesitated. Her father wouldn't be pleased to see her on the arm of another man when she was supposed to be charming the king. Especially as he hadn't been introduced to her and she had no idea who he was. Though, that was half the fun of a masquerade ball. Being strange and mysterious was not only allowed but encouraged. And besides, what better way to get the king's attention than to be seen with another man? Especially, one as striking as the man before her. One could hardly help but notice him. And men were so prone to jealousy. Or at least a strong desire to mark their territory. How could the king help but want to discover the identity of the jeweled peacock who'd entered the ball on the arm of a towering lion? That would make her father happy.

She took his arm and smiled up at him. "That would be most welcome."

. . .

Malcolm MacGregor tucked the woman's soft hand into the crook of his arm and led her toward the ballroom. He hadn't been looking forward to tonight's revelries. Truth be told, he was heartily sick of court and wanted nothing more than to return home. But he, laird of Glenlyon, had been summoned by his king to hopefully put the Campbell matter to rest once and for all. The traitorous clan had been doing their level best to roust his kin from their lands for as long as anyone could remember. But lately, their attacks had been more open, more brazen. And more destructive.

They'd destroyed a village only a fortnight before, burning it to the ground, stealing many of the cattle and livestock they'd found in the fields nearby, and had made off with two young women. The women had been recovered, thankfully, before too much damage could occur, and Malcolm had brought at least a few of the culprits to court with him. They were currently rotting in the dungeons until he could present his case to Charles. The miscreants would provide proof that the Campbells were the instigators of the feud between the clans. Old Angus Campbell wouldn't be able to argue his way out of this one, not with Campbell men who'd been caught in the act in Malcolm's custody.

The ball was merely another obstacle forcing him to wait an additional day to see the king. He wouldn't have attended at all, but he was sure Campbell would be there and he couldn't give the man an opportunity to poison the king more than he already had. But, now, perhaps the night would prove diverting.

He found he enjoyed the bit of anonymity the masked ball afforded him. The MacGregors had not been welcome at court for longer than most could remember. At least not under the name of MacGregor. The king's reversal of the laws against the clan and use of the clan name were still new enough that people had not yet grown used to the sight of an actual MacGregor wandering freely about the palace. He'd grown heartily sick of the looks and whispers. And glad he needn't endure them from the lady he'd so fortuitously run into.

The woman at his side was lovely, the blue of her gown and the jewels in her mask setting off the deep sapphire of her eyes. Her form pleased him as well. Her dress hung on her becomingly, framing her ample bosom nicely, instead of making it appear as though she were an over-risen loaf of bread stuffed into a baking pan. Though not so thin that she looked as though a stiff breeze could blow her away. She'd obviously spent most of her life coddled indoors, but there was still a sturdiness to her that many of the court's women lacked. Except, the last time he'd commented on a woman's sturdiness, he'd received a palm to his face, so that thought he'd keep to himself.

He brought them around to a side door. She looked up at him in question and he winked at her. "Best if we sneak in the back as we are most certainly late. The king has already arrived." He gestured to the bedecked figure of the king sitting on a dais above the dancers.

"Good thinking," she murmured. "That means my father is also here, most likely wondering where I am. And not very patiently, I'd wager."

"As ye're likely already in a spot of trouble, shall we give him the slip a mite longer?" He gave her a wicked grin which made her laugh, a delightful trill that brought a smile to his lips.

"Might as well," she agreed. "If I'm to be reprimanded, I might as well have a bit of fun for the trouble."

They slipped in among the crowd, milling around the revelers.

"Dance with me," he said, as the musicians began another song. He whisked her onto the floor, not waiting for her response. She lined up with the other dancers, the smile playing about her lips sending his heart into a staccato beat.

"I don't think I've ever met anyone like you," she said when the dance brought them together.

"No?" he asked, letting his thumb caress the back of her hand until the steps of the dance required him to move away.

A few more spins and they were face-to-face again. "No. You're…larger than life."

He chuckled, the sound almost rusty in his throat. There had not been many moments of laughter in his life, lately. "Aye, well, I suppose I am a wee bigger than average."

He glanced around at their company. He towered over the women, of course. But few men matched his height, even in the heeled shoes that were the rage of current fashion.

She laughed again and gripped his hand as the dance led them forward a few steps. "That's not what I meant."

The dance spun them away from each other, and then the music ended, and they bowed.

"What did ye mean?" he asked, taking her hand again.

Her gaze dropped from his and focused a few inches lower, on his lips, he thought. She wet her own, and the sight of her tongue darting over her full, kissable lips had his belly tightening against the sudden burst of desire.

Then her attention was drawn to someone behind him, and her face paled slightly.

"My father," she murmured.

Malcolm didn't look back to see who the man was. He simply tucked her hand back on his arm and led her off the dance floor, blending into the crowd once again. Though she'd been right about one thing...he was a big beast of a man and staying hidden wasn't the easiest task. Another large room adjacent to the one they'd departed had been set up as a refreshment area, with tables of delectable treats and drinks—and several small curtained alcoves perfect for losing oneself in.

He whisked her into one before she could protest.

"I think ye'll be safe from fearsome fathers in here, my lady," he said.

"Thank you. I was about to suggest it."

He glanced at her in surprise, and she boldly met his gaze. "Well now, if ye're in the habit of suggesting that strange men spirit ye away into secluded alcoves, perhaps your father has reason to fear."

She shrugged and looked up at him from beneath thick, dark lashes. "Perhaps."

"Is this something ye do often?" he asked, finding he didn't like the idea of her hiding away with other men. A ridiculous feeling, as he'd only just met her and hadn't even seen her face yet, let alone gotten to know her well enough to warrant a little jealousy. Nevertheless, there it was. He stepped closer. She didn't back away.

"No. I'm usually very well behaved."

"*Hmm.*" He reached out and traced the outline of her mask. "Mayhap hiding your identity is giving ye courage where ye had none."

She squared her shoulders. "I have always been courageous, my lord. I've simply been more…cautious, you could say."

"And now?"

She shrugged and the movement caused her gown to dip tantalizingly low. He bit his lip to keep from groaning and trailed a hand up her arm.

"Now, I'm looking for a little adventure," she said. "I'm tired of being cautious."

"Well, you're ambitious, I'll give ye that. Most women would start with something small. A brisk walk in the garden. Or serving chocolate at tea time instead of tea." He mock gasped, and she chuckled. Not a giggle as he'd expected, but a husky, throaty laugh that reached out and squeezed all the air from his lungs. This was no green girl he flirted with. Oh, she was inexperienced, for sure. But she wasn't a child, either.

"Do you find ambition attractive in a woman, my lord?"

"I think it depends on the person. Woman or man, ambition can be a great strength to be admired, or a weakness to be despised."

"And in me? Do you find me attractive?" She took a step closer. Only inches separated them now. Mere wisps of air that he could cross without any effort. She was almost in his arms already. He only had to reach out…and take her.

His heart punched his chest. This brazen little lassie had no idea what she was doing to him. Perhaps he should enlighten her.

He traced her full bottom lip with his thumb. "I think ye already ken that I do."

Before he could talk himself out of it, he pulled her close and leaned down to taste her delectable mouth. He brushed his lips lightly across hers, gauging her reaction. She rose to her tip toes and kissed him back, pressing her lips firmly to his.

Within moments, he had her pressed against the wall of the alcove, their arms wrapped around each other, lips moving and tasting until they were both breathless.

"My lady," a voice hissed from the other side of the curtain. "My lady!"

The woman in his arms jerked back, her eyes dazed and bright with passion. She blinked a few times, and then her eyes widened, and she flicked back the corner of the curtain.

"Berta, what is it?"

"Your father, my lady. He's asking for you. I don't think I can stall him anymore."

She nodded and waved her maid off before turning back to him. "I'm afraid I need to leave, my lord." She stepped out of the alcove before he could respond. "I thank you for the adventure."

She gave him a brilliant grin and a wave and then was gone, leaving him laughing but alone in the alcove.

He would have to find out who she was before he left court. He'd been a happy bachelor, for the most part, for years. But a woman like her might be enough to make him reconsider his situation. If he could find her again.

His amusement died away when he remembered his purpose for being at court. He sighed and brushed at his clothes, making sure everything was put back to rights. There was a rather large and dangerous problem that needed to be taken care of before he left. Once that was handled, then he could turn his mind back to more…adventurous things.

Chapter Two

Malcolm's head pounded. The ball had rambled on until the wee hours of the morning, and the prospect of the meeting which faced him didn't help matters. He forced his fists to relax and tried to remember where he was. The court of Charles II was jovial, often downright lecherous. But there were some things even Charles wouldn't stand for, and murdering one of his subjects in the royal audience chambers right in front of him was one of them. Instead, Malcolm jammed his hand through his hair, pulling hard enough to hurt. Pain was good. Distracting.

He ran his hand through his hair once more. It was a habit he tried to avoid as it tended to make him look like a mutt with a coat full of burrs. But it was either attack his own hair or his rival, Angus Campbell. And attacking his hair wouldn't get him slaughtered for brawling in front of the king. Though judging by Charles's expression he was almost as ready to commit violence as Malcolm.

Campbell either didn't notice or didn't care about Charles's rapidly fraying patience or Malcolm's tenuous hold on his rage. Instead, he pressed on with his complaints.

"You, MacGregors, or whatever most of your clan is calling itself these days, are all the same. Cattle rustlers and deer poachers, all! And you are the worst of the lot!" he said, jabbing a finger toward Malcolm.

"Now, that is a lie!" Malcolm said, jumping from his seat. He pointed at Campbell. "It's you and yer men that have been raiding our lands. Three already this month."

"What lands? Ye've little enough left to the name MacGregor after all these years the clan's been outlawed. And what ye do have isna worth my time, even if I were to condone these supposed attacks."

"I find that interesting, since the men I captured and brought with me today have bog myrtle in their bonnets and that rotten Campbell stench on their skin!"

Campbell's jaw dropped, and Malcolm barely refrained from laughing at the shock in the man's beady eyes. He hadn't known Malcolm had brought prisoners with him. Good. Hard to deny his men were raiding MacGregor lands when he had those men in custody. Proudly sporting the symbol of their clan, no less. Malcolm and his men retaliated when necessary, but they didn't go about proclaiming who they were while they did it. A logical precaution should any of them be captured. If there was one thing MacGregors were good at, it was surviving.

"I've no doubt ye're lying about the why and how ye took my men, but even if it's the truth, which isna likely, any so-called raids on our part would have only been enacted in retribution for the three you led against me!"

Malcolm leaned on the table, getting as close to Campbell as he could without removing the furniture in his path. "I've never made a move against ye that wasna provoked."

"I find that hard to believe, as I've never made a move to provoke you, yet ye seem hell bent on destroying me, nevertheless!"

It was Malcolm's turn to be stunned with surprise. "Never made a move? Campbells have been stealing our lands and hunting MacGregors since before our grandfathers were born."

"If such acts ever occurred, they were fully sanctioned by law!"

"Aye, but no longer! Those laws have been repealed, yet yer men continue to run off MacGregor cattle, steal or ruin crops for sport, and in at least two villages, a few farmers' daughters, as well. Did ye really think we'd stand by and let ye wreak havoc on what little we have left to us?"

"Wreak havoc, is it? We've done no more than you've done to us. Actually, a great deal less. We've done nothing to warrant these ceaseless attacks—"

"Aye, ye have and ye know it and ye've not paid half the price I could have extracted." Malcolm's hand clenched into fists at his sides. "Trust me, ye old fool, if I came against ye in earnest, you'd know it."

"Why you…" Campbell sputtered. "Ye heard him," he said, addressing the others in the room. "Ye heard his threats!" He turned back to Malcolm. "I'll bring the full force of the law down on ye and yer heathen kinsmen. I'll see yer entire clan outlawed again, as ye should be. That you have the audacity to stand there and call yerself a MacGregor at all is—"

"Enough!" Charles roared.

They all froze and stared at the king. Malcolm was pleased to see Campbell's normally splotchy complexion drained of all color while he waited for Charles to vent his wrath.

"Campbell, I'll not hear another word about the past sins of the MacGregor clan. The acts against them were repealed when I regained my throne. They earned their reinstatement and the repeal of the proscription against their name due to their valor in the battles that helped defeat my enemies.

Your clan, as I recall, did not do much to distinguish itself. Reminding me of that failure and questioning my judgment in the MacGregors' reinstatement would not be wise on your part."

"Pardon, Your Majesty. I did not mean to—"

Charles held up an impatient hand to stop Campbell's rambling. Then he turned to Malcolm.

"And you…I may count you as friend, but that does not mean I wish to be subject to your squabbles with your neighbors. I have enough to deal with in running the rest of this kingdom."

Malcolm bowed his head, embarrassed he'd allowed the old man to rile him so in front of his monarch. He did consider Charles a friend, for all that he was English. He'd spent some time in exile with him, bolstered support at home when he could, because English or not, anyone was better than that bastard Cromwell. He had fought valiantly to put Charles back on the throne. Fortunately, Charles counted him as a friend and ally. But that did not excuse bickering like old women in front of his king. His mother would have boxed his ears, and rightly so.

But his temper was quick to explode these days, mostly because of the gentleman sitting opposite him falsely proclaiming his innocence. The fact he could do so with a straight face, when Malcolm knew for a fact that Campbell and his men were behind the raids that had weakened his holdings, and robbed him of his family, was more than he could tolerate.

Still, he bit his tongue and waited for Charles to continue. Charles motioned for them both to sit. Malcolm did so gratefully. The king was correct. The MacGregors were in a precarious position. Their name and some of their lands might have been reverted to them by Charles's generosity, but not everyone was happy about it. While many clans had opened their arms to the MacGregors and sheltered them during the decades after their downfall, others, with the Campbells in the forefront, had reveled in the misfortune of their enemy. The retraction of the laws permitting the persecution of the Clan MacGregor was still too new. Malcolm would do well to tread lightly.

"I need my kingdom united and at peace. I have troubles enough here in London. The last thing I need is to be constantly hearing petitions from Scotland on matters I have already settled. So. I have a solution. One that I'm quite sure you will both protest, but it will put an end to this ceaseless fighting, once and for all, and I'm not inclined to hear any pleading to the contrary."

Malcolm clenched his jaw to keep his objection from erupting. He had a fair feeling he knew what was coming, and the notion made his stomach twist. Charles's first words confirmed his fears.

"Campbell, you have an unmarried daughter, I believe. How old is she now?"

If he hadn't been busy trying to keep down his breakfast, Malcolm would have laughed at the expression on Campbell's face. Seems like the old man had come to the same conclusion Malcolm had, and didn't like it any better.

"Yes, Your Majesty. Sorcha. She is twenty years, sire."

Malcolm's stomach lurched. He could never be with a Campbell. Not that one would ever want to be with him.

"Good." Charles nodded, oblivious to the turmoil going on inside Malcolm's head. Then the king turned to Malcolm. "And you, my lord, have no wife."

"My life isna well suited to a wife, sire. Glenlyon is no' so large an estate as to attract most women, especially when they have to take me with it." Not that he wanted to remain unmarried forever.

In truth, a wife would be useful, especially if she came

with a large dowry. He had estates that needed tending. And would like an heir someday. A task that would be made easier if he were wed to a warm and willing wife...one perhaps like the firebrand he'd held in his arms the night before. The memory of her soft body pressed against him while her lips moved tantalizingly beneath his was one he'd not forget any time soon.

But not a Campbell wife. She'd be more likely to slit his throat while he slept than keep his home in order and bear his children.

Charles didn't seem to agree. He waved off Malcolm's concern. "Nonsense. I'm sure many find you dashing."

"Your Majesty..." he said.

Charles ignored him. "The feuding must end. And what better way to accomplish such a task than by uniting your families through marriage?"

"Sire, my daughter is headstrong. She'll not..."

"She will, if her king decrees it," Charles said, pinning Campbell with a glare that left the older man no room to complain. Campbell nodded his head reluctantly, as if forcing the movement through thick molasses.

Malcolm didn't bother to argue further. There would be no changing Charles's mind. In a similar circumstance, Malcolm would have likely offered the same solution. As long as he was not the intended bridegroom.

Charles looked between the two of them and nodded. "Excellent. The marriage will take place in two hours in my private chapel."

Both men erupted with a flurry of protests. Malcolm's stomach twisted. It was too soon. He couldn't go through with it. There was no time to prepare. Or escape.

Charles held up his hand again. "I want this settled. I have no intention of sending you back to your lands with matters as they currently stand. And as I have no wish to have you hanging about my court trying your damndest to kill each other, we will have this done with. I have already had the contracts drawn up, so no time will be wasted on further arguments. You need do nothing but show up at church in two hours."

Charles rose. The audience was over. Malcolm bowed, though his head pounded with the effort it took to keep his tongue leashed. A thousand solutions ran through his mind, but he discarded each of them. Disobeying would have harsh consequences, and not only for himself. His clan had only recently rediscovered the favor of the king. He was in no position to complain.

In fact, Charles had shown him great esteem in giving him Sorcha Campbell's hand.

Yet it was the last thing he wanted. Putting aside the fact that he'd be dooming a woman who could have her pick of court to a life shackled to the Lion of Glenlyon, as the villagers called him—she was a Campbell. If Malcolm woke from their wedding night with his head still attached to his body, he'd be amazed. He could but hope his head was all she chopped off.

Malcolm had no intention of remaining in Campbell's presence to hear more of his threats and lies. As soon as the king's entourage disappeared around the corner, Malcolm turned to make his own retreat.

"MacGregor!"

Malcolm paused, glancing over his shoulder at his enemy. "I've no more time for this," he said, the ache in his head intensifying. Ever since his encounter with the sword that nearly cleft his skull in two, his headaches had grown more and more troublesome. The only thing he wanted at the moment was a cold cloth over his eyes and a glass full of whisky in his hand.

"She's my only daughter."

Malcolm's shoulders slumped in defeat. Those weren't

the words of a belligerent enemy. They were the words of a father, worried for his child.

"I've no more wish for this than you do, Campbell. But it seems we have little choice in the matter."

The old man's face puckered with loathing as he looked Malcolm up and down. "I've turned away every man who has asked for her hand. Lords, counts, earls. None of them were good enough for her. She was meant for greater things. A duke, at the very least. If not a prince. And now I'm forced to give her over to you. To watch the flower I cultivated so carefully be destroyed by the devil himself."

Malcolm kept a tight rein on his anger. The man might be a liar, a thief, a murderer, and probably much worse. But he seemed to genuinely care for his daughter. Or at least for the connections her marriage might have brought him. And to be honest, Malcolm couldn't blame the man for despising the choice before them. He'd never hand his daughter over to a man like himself.

"I may be yer enemy, Campbell. But I have no intentions of making yer daughter pay for the sins of her father. I swear on my honor, she willna come to harm while under my protection."

Campbell's jaw clenched, and Malcolm could only imagine what thoughts were running through the man's head. Finally, he jerked his head in a quick nod and stalked from the room.

Malcolm sighed and rubbed his hand over his face. It looked like he had a wedding to prepare for.

Chapter Three

Sorcha had twisted the edges of her fan until it would no longer open and had nearly worn a path in the polished wood of the hallway that led to the king's chambers, and still her father hadn't made an appearance. He had been closeted away with the king and Laird Glenlyon for the better part of two hours. She knew that her father had meant to petition the king against Glenlyon but frankly, Sorcha had thought him daft for trying. Everyone knew the Scottish laird and the English king had become fast friends during the king's exile. With the entire MacGregor clan back in favor after wallowing as outlaws for so many years, bringing a petition against them now wasn't the wisest choice her father could have made.

Then again, something had to be done. The raids and skirmishes needed to stop before there was nothing left of either clan. And the Campbells were well known for using their knowledge of the law to bring down their enemies. Despite Glenlyon's friendship with the king, there was a chance that her father had found a solution to their problems.

What she had never considered was that she might play a

role. Until the king had passed by several minutes prior and given her a benevolent smile before walking on. Now, she must wait for her father to fetch her, her stomach in knots and her fan in shreds. As a woman, there were very few ways in which she could be of service in situations such as these. And none of them were to her liking. Yet she couldn't fathom that her father would agree to the most likely resolution.

Finally, she caught sight of him striding angrily from the king's chambers. The anxiety in her gut increased to the point of pain.

"Father," she said, stepping into his path when it looked like he'd pass her by. "What news?"

He glowered at her. "I will discuss it with you privately."

Before she could protest and insist he tell her right then, a tall figure stopped beside them. Sorcha glanced up and saw the strange amber eyes of the man she'd met before the ball. The one she'd danced with. Laughed with. Who'd swept her into an alcove and into his arms and...

She halted that thought before it could take root, her cheeks flaming.

Someone whispered behind her. "The Lion."

Sorcha's head jerked up, looking at him anew. *He* was the MacGregor laird tormenting her father? The one they called the Lion? She could see why. He exuded sheer strength and virility. Something he probably needed, as he rode against her kinsmen in the dark of night. Her eyes narrowed. Had he known who she was when he'd taken such liberties with her in that alcove? Had it been part of some sick revenge scheme?

He didn't flinch beneath her heated gaze. Not that she'd expected him to. Everything about him screamed danger.

Though the court was crowded that day, everyone gave him a wide berth, as though there were a protective circle surrounding him that only the bravest penetrated. The only exception to this was another Scot who stood beside him.

That one didn't seem nearly as threatening. He certainly had the size to be imposing but everyone seemed to diminish in stature compared to the Lion. The man's passive gaze swept over her. He gave her a brief nod, and then he went back to surveying the room, as though on the lookout for danger.

"Is this her?" the Lion asked, his deep voice rumbling from his chest as though he didn't really want to know the answer.

Sorcha's father drew up to his full height, rage mottling his cheeks. But when he spoke, his words were civil enough, even if there was an undercurrent of fury beneath them.

"Yes, this is my daughter. Sorcha, this is Malcolm MacGregor, Laird Glenlyon."

Sorcha dropped into the curtsy that was expected of her as a polite member of court, even as his name seared its way into her mind. Showing such respect to a MacGregor nearly made her knees lock up. Or perhaps it was the memory of his lips on hers and the way she'd felt cradled in his arms that made her head faint. She'd enjoyed his touch. Before she'd known who he was.

If the beastly laird before her noticed her stiffness, he chose not to remark on it. Instead, those cold, glittering eyes of his looked her up and down again.

"Aye, I suppose she'll do."

Then he turned on his heel and walked away, leaving her confused and angry and her father sputtering with rage.

"What did he mean by that?" she asked him. "I'll do for what?"

Her father didn't answer her, but instead strode off in the direction of their chambers.

"Father," she insisted, her gut twisting inside her. "What did he mean?" She was fairly certain she knew exactly what he meant and if her father didn't dissuade her of the notion immediately, she greatly feared she'd be sick.

"Not here!" he said over his shoulder as she rushed to keep pace with him.

She gathered her skirts and hurried along, only barely managing to keep from pestering him more. That was not the way to get information from her father.

When they reached her father's chamber he marched inside, grabbed his wig from his head and threw it on the nearest table, and slumped into his favorite chair by the fireplace. His servant had a glass of whisky in his hand before he'd even finished getting settled.

He took a deep drink and sat back with a sigh.

"Father?" she asked, taking care to keep her voice low and sweet.

He glanced at her briefly and then returned his gaze to the fire.

"You are to be wed." He took another drink.

Sorcha took a step away from him. It was no more than she'd expected. Yet, still, she hadn't been prepared. "Wed? But we've heard nothing…"

"The king has decreed that to put an end to the feud between our clan and the MacGregors—"

"Don't," she said, her voice hardly more than a whisper. "Don't say it."

Her father ignored her. "Ye're to wed the Laird of Glenlyon."

Her heart lurched in a desperate attempt to escape from her chest and render her dead. For a breathtaking moment, exhileration coursed through her. She'd seen more than a few friends married off to whomever their families felt would be the most advantageous. The man's age and physical appearance was rarely a consideration in these matters. Only the size of his estate and the prestige of his title. So the prospect of marrying a healthy, handsome warrior who wasn't twice her age momentarily piqued her interest. Especially, with the memory of their moments in the alcove still burning hot through her blood.

And then it sank in. This wasn't just any man. He was a MacGregor. Better she were dead than to live life as the wife of that man. Or any MacGregor.

"But…I…" She couldn't form a coherent enough thought to get out of her mouth. So instead, she paced.

Back and forth in front of her father's chair until finally, he sighed and rubbed his forehead. "Sit down, child. Ye're making my head ache something fierce."

Sorcha tried not to glare at him. Angering him wouldn't help her now. Her father despised strong-willed, outspoken women. To be fair, he wasn't fond of men whose opinions ran contrary to his own, either. So she generally tried to sweet talk her way into her father's good graces. But the fury and fear running through her veins at her father's news had her mind in turmoil. Still, railing at him would gain her nothing. Different tactics were needed.

"Father, please," she said, dropping to her knees in front of him. She took his hands in hers and looked up into his eyes, hoping she presented the picture of poised perfection, instead of the wild woman that was seconds from breaking free. "Please, you can't make me marry him. I don't even know him."

For a moment her father's eyes softened. Then his jaw clenched, and he withdrew his hands with a *humpf* of irritation.

"What has that to do with anything? It's already been decided. There is nothing I can do about it now."

Sorcha pushed back to her feet, resuming her pacing in an attempt to keep calm. "But he's a MacGregor! He'll probably put the horse whip to me every day just to watch a Campbell scream. You can't really mean to abandon me with him."

Her father frowned. "For all that MacGregor is a right bastard, I dinna think he'll mistreat you. I wouldna trust him with my cattle if I had the oath of the all the saints themselves, but…"

"But you'll trust him with your daughter?"

He sighed again. "The king himself has decreed this marriage will take place. He's even holding it in his private chapel, and he himself will attend. It's a great honor, Sorcha."

"Fine. Then you wed him!"

"That's enough!" her father said, surging up from his chair.

Sorcha flinched. She knew she'd gone too far before the words had left her mouth, but she couldn't help but say them.

"I dinna want ye to marry him anymore than you do, but ye have no choice in the matter so I'll hear nae more about it! The wedding is in two hours."

Sorcha gasped. "So soon? Why?"

Her father snorted. "The king probably wants it done before the groom disappears."

She frowned at that, unable to stop the twinge of hurt pride. "He truly finds me so repugnant?"

Her father's eyebrows rose. "As far as I know, he'd never seen ye until a few moments ago."

Sorcha bit her lip. That was true…except for those moments at the ball…

Her father didn't notice her distraction. "Ye're a Campbell. That's enough to make him loathe even the thought of you."

"And yet you'll allow him to marry me and do what he will with me."

"Ye speak as though I have a choice in the matter." He frowned again. "As I said, I dinna think he'll harm you. No matter his feelings about our clan, he's never had the reputation of a man who is cruel to women. Quite the opposite, actually. And he's given me his word of honor no harm will come to you."

"But Father—"

He waved her off. "Two hours, in the king's private apartments. I'll be back to fetch you. See that ye're ready. And wear yer finest gown. I might want nothing to do with this marriage, but I willna have it said that my daughter went before the king in anything but the finest money could buy."

He strode to the door and was gone before Sorcha could say another word. Not that it would have helped.

The moment the door closed Sorcha flung herself on her bed and buried her head in the pillows. Not to stifle her sobs, but to muffle her furious screams.

"Oh my lady," her maid said, sitting on her bed and petting her hair. "Perhaps it's not so bad. Just think, the king himself will attend your wedding!"

That made Sorcha groan louder.

"That only makes it more difficult to escape," she mumbled into her pillow.

"Perhaps not."

Sorcha peeked an eye out from the pillow. "What do you mean?"

"Your father and the king said you had to marry him. They didn't say you had to *stay* married to him."

"I don't understand. Once we are married, we are joined until one of us dies. I'm certainly not going to hasten my own end. And despite the near certainty that this man is a brutal bastard of the lowest degree, I can't justify killing him."

"I'm not speaking of murder, my lady."

"Then I don't understand."

Her maid smiled. "Your marriage could be annulled, my lady. It's not easy. However, there are circumstances…"

Sorcha sat up, a small spark of hope blossoming in her chest. "That…that might actually work. Though…I couldn't make it seem as though I were at fault. Escaping the marriage would do no good if I bring the king's wrath down on my family to do it. But if he were unable to…to…"

"Perform his husbandly duties?" her maid supplied.

Sorcha's cheeks flamed but she nodded. "I could hardly be faulted if I was there and willing. And in the morning when I proclaim that nothing occurred due to his inability, then we'll have grounds to sue for an annulment. The scandal alone might make him agree, even if he won't agree to the examination to prove his impotence. And I'll be free!"

She hugged her maid tight. "Come. We have much to do and very little time."

Chapter Four

Malcolm paced in his chamber, pausing every now and then to gulp down another tumbler of whisky. He still couldn't believe he was in this mess. When he had answered Charles's summons he'd never dreamed that he'd end up with some cursed Campbell bride foisted on him.

"Ye might want to go easy on that."

Malcolm glanced over at his cousin, John, and glared. "It's the only damn thing keeping me from tearing this palace down brick by brick."

"Oh, aye," John said. "Because whisky only ever calms a riled up Scot. That makes sense."

Malcolm snorted and put down his glass. His cousin was right. Then again, he usually was. John had been Malcolm's friend and ally their whole lives. When Malcolm's father had been killed in a skirmish against the Campbells, John's father had stepped in and been the father-figure in Malcolm's life. Taught him to fight and strategize. Raised him right along with his own son. John was more brother to Malcolm than anything else and, more often than not, the voice of reason when Malcolm was ready to jump straight into battle.

"Marriage might not be the worst thing in the world, ye know," John said.

Malcolm's eyebrow raised. Then again, John wasn't *always* right.

"Ye say that because it isna you being forced to marry the Campbell creature."

John shrugged. "True. But there's no getting out of it, Cousin. It's an order from yer king who is doing you the honor of attending your wedding."

Malcolm snorted. "Some honor."

John frowned at that. "It *is* an honor. And if ye treat it as anything less, you'll be the one who'll provoke Charles's ire. Our clan has only recently been restored to favor. Would ye risk all that now just to avoid marrying this girl?"

Malcolm frowned deeper. What a difference a night makes. When he'd first met her, he'd have risked much for the chance to get closer to her. She was spirited and beautiful, with a passion lurking beneath the surface that called to him to release it. If the king had commanded him to marry her right then, he'd have happily dragged her off to the chapel and then to his bed.

But that had been before. Before he knew who she was. Who had raised her. She might be all the things he'd thought when he'd met her. But she was also a Campbell. And an attraction sparked while incognito wouldn't erase centuries of hating anyone with the name of MacGregor. It wouldn't change the treachery and deceit that seemed to be ingrained in every Campbell he'd ever come across.

Yet his clan had come too far to destroy their turn in favor now. "No. I wouldna risk the well being of the clan. But that doesna mean I have to go to my marriage bed whistling like a merry fool when I'm being saddled with a bride who'll be only too happy to slit my throat the moment I have the misfortune of falling asleep in her presence."

"Well, I'm no' saying ye shouldna sleep with one eye open. But I'm also no' saying there's any need for ye to stay married, either."

"What?"

"Charles has ordered ye to wed the woman. But he canna force ye to remain in her company. Ye might even be able to get the marriage annulled, if you can prove her insane."

"That probably wouldna be too difficult. Considering her kin, I'm fairly certain the woman *is* daft." Malcolm stopped his pacing and sat in the chair across from his cousin. "Failing that, I suppose I could drive her away. Inspire her to insist upon separate living quarters. It would be preferable to living wi' the woman. She might even agree to the scandal of a divorce if I make myself…intolerable enough. Though I dinna see how that will get me out of the marriage while retaining Charles's favor."

John shrugged. "Just be sure not to consummate the marriage. It might not hinder the legal proceedings much but it would certainly complicate things."

Malcolm's eyebrows rose, a slow smile spreading across his face. "Aye. Charles may not be pleased, but he canna force me to rape an unwilling woman. Though…" he frowned again, thoughts of her blushed cheeks and faint gasps when he had kissed her running through his head. "What if she *is* willing?"

This time John's eyebrows rose. "A Campbell woman being told she must marry a man who she's been taught her whole life is the monstrous enemy? With naught but an hour or two to get used to the idea? I guarantee she willna be willing. Then perhaps ye could discover she is diseased or addled in the brain with some affliction."

"And how do I discover that?"

John shrugged. "Proving her mad might take a bit more time. Some physical ailment might be more efficient. Nettle oil would raise a nice rash, make it appear as though she were suffering from some malady."

Malcolm's eyes widened, and he cursed under his breath. "I'm no' going to poison the lass!"

John shrugged again. "If ye object to that, ye could claim you took her to bed only to discover she was no virgin. Sue for annulment on the grounds of deceit."

Malcolm frowned at that. "It would be my word against hers. And I dinna want to ruin her chances for remarriage. I just dinna want to be shackled to the woman myself."

"Ye might not be able to avoid ruining her. There will certainly be a scandal. But if ye want to extract yourself and leave her reputation somewhat intact, then I suppose ye'll have to be yer usual delightful self and drive the woman away with naught but the pleasure of your company."

Malcolm snorted. "Wi' friends like you to vouch for my character, the poor lass will no doubt run screaming from the chapel the moment the vows are spoken. If not before."

He sighed and rubbed his hand over his face. There was naught to do but wed the woman and unleash his worst behavior in the hopes of chasing her off at the earliest possible moment. A small part of him pitied her. It was bad enough for him. But for a woman to be forced to marry a man she didn't know, one she'd been taught to fear… That fact didn't sit well with him, but if it would work to his purpose, he'd have to live with it. Pity or not, he'd not spend the rest of his life bound to a woman who hated him.

"Very well. I'll outwardly accept the marriage and then do my damned level best to sabotage it. The king canna fault me if the chit is the one who runs off. So…" he stood up and slapped his leg. "It seems I have a wedding to prepare for."

It wasn't the best plan in the world, but it was better than being tied to his worst enemy's daughter for the rest of his life. Which, he was sure, would be considerably shortened if his bride and her kin had any say in the matter.

"Ye'd better make quick work of it or ye'll be late. Now, let's hope yer plan works. With any luck, ye'll never even make it back to your apartments."

"Aye. But ye might want to go through my belongings and hide anything lethal on the chance that we do."

John's laughter rang through the chamber. "I will see that it's done."

An hour later, Malcolm stood freshly washed and dressed in his finest. He'd have preferred a sprig of Scottish pine tucked in his bonnet, but as they were several days journey from the nearest tree, he'd had to make do with a silver brooch representation instead. He tried not to fidget as he stood before the priest, waiting for his bride to appear. Charles sat to one side, his patience growing thinner by the moment. Campbell had bent to offer yet another apology for his daughter's tardiness when she was finally ushered in.

He didn't know what he'd expected. That she'd suddenly changed appearance now that he knew she was a Campbell? That those striking blue eyes framed by dark lashes and lusciously kissable lips had miraculously transformed into those that resembled her father more, he supposed, with his long face and crooked teeth and thin carrot-colored hair.

Malcolm had often found tales of a woman's beauty were greatly exaggerated. But not this time. Angus Campbell's daughter was a vision of loveliness. She must have her mother's coloring, with her pale skin smooth and unblemished, like the feathers of a pure white dove. Her ebony hair was gathered in rich, dark ringlets on either side of her head, framing her face. Her eyes... He waited for her to turn to him so he could get a glimpse of those eyes that had captivated him since the moment he'd seen them framed by her gilded mask.

For a split second he saw them, a bright, rich blue that reminded him of a spring sky over the loch near his home. Eyes he could fall into, drown in. Until they caught sight of him and widened. She took a step back, bumping into the liveried servant who stood attention at the door and causing a minor scuffle as the poor boy righted himself and retook his post. Then those bright eyes of hers met Malcolm's and immediately narrowed. Her hands clenched fistfuls of her skirts so tightly her knuckles stood out in stark, white relief against the deep blue of her gown. She took a deep breath and visibly straightened. Like she was calling on all her strength to do something unpleasant. To marry him. *He* was the unpleasant task. The sacrifice she was making for her king and clan.

He didn't want to marry her, either, despite the supposed honor he'd been shown. He knew she was wealthy, titled, and she certainly lived up to the accounts of her extraordinary beauty with her raven hair and flashing blue eyes. Many men had tried and failed to capture the woman's heart. Or, at least, the approval of her father. He tried to keep in mind that such a match was extremely advantageous. But it still rankled.

Despite his feelings on the matter, he was there, and prepared to be civil. Unlike his blushing bride. The fact that she didn't bother to hide her revulsion, especially after her flirtatious display at the ball, erased what little sympathy he might have had for her. Along with any guilt he may have had for his plans to sabotage their marriage. Now, he was more certain than ever of his course of action.

It would be a kindness to her, really. She obviously didn't want to be saddled with him anymore than he wanted to be bound to her. A flash of memory from the alcove, her quiet moans as his lips moved over hers, tightened things low and deep in his belly. He clenched his jaw and did his best to force those thoughts from his mind. His body might lust after her. The rational part of him knew better.

He kept his gaze on her as she marched stoically up the aisle to where he and the others were gathered. Her maid fluttered behind her, reaching out to straighten the hem of her gown a few times.

He had to admit, she'd at least dressed for the occasion. The sapphire hue of her gown complemented her perfectly. Truly, she was everything a man could desire in a wife, at least in appearance. If he had, in any way, desired a wife. But the eyes she finally raised to him were full of anger. And a touch of fear. It was nothing more than he expected, but stung none the less.

Well, no matter her feelings on the matter, they were both stuck.

Charles clapped his hands, and the priest began intoning the words that were meant to tie him to this woman for the rest of their lives. Hopefully, if he had anything to say about it, their union would be considerably shorter.

At the priest's directions, Malcolm took Sorcha's trembling hand in his. He couldn't stop the rush of tenderness that spread through him at that small sign of her anxiety. He gently squeezed her hand and she glanced up at him, her piercing eyes burning into his from under dark lashes. She let out a tremulous breath and her hand steadied. When it came time for her to recite her vows, she did so with a clear, if quiet, voice.

The priest blessed the delicate gold band set with a small pearl that Charles had provided for the occasion. No doubt to ensure there would be no further attempts to delay the ceremony. Malcolm took the ring and slipped it onto her finger. Her hand had steadied and rested easily in his. Perhaps she wasn't as averse to the union as he'd thought. Other than the fact of his clan, Malcolm was a fair match for her. Nephew to the MacGregor chieftain, and laird of a sizeable estate.

And she'd seemed interested enough before.

Of course, his land was buried in the Highlands, far from the cities Sorcha was more familiar with. And the keep he called home was in desperate need of repair. Still, he had much to offer a woman.

Though apparently not the lady before him. Ceremony over, Malcolm leaned in to kiss his bride, and she recoiled as if a snake had presented its fangs for her touch. He should have known better than to think, even for a moment, this marriage could be anything other than doomed.

Very well. Let the battle begin.

He pressed a chaste and heartily unwelcome kiss to Sorcha's cheek, though she jerked away so his lips only glanced off her skin.

"Ah, come now, my lord. Give her a proper kiss!" the king said.

Malcolm looked down at her, and she gave a subtle shake of her head. "Don't you dare," she whispered.

"Sorry," he murmured back, wrapping an arm about her waist to draw her to him. "The king commands."

She put her hands on his chest but he bent and captured her lips before she could say anything else. Under normal circumstances, he wouldn't have forced the issue, but king's orders were king's orders. And he couldn't erase the memory of her sweet lips from the night of the ball. Perhaps, if he reminded her of how much she'd enjoyed their interlude she wouldn't be so reluctant to accept him as her husband.

Her fingers tightened in his coat, and for a moment, she responded to him, her lips moving beneath his. Then a spattering of applause broke out in the chamber, and she seemed to remember where she was, what was happening. Her foot came down on his with enough force to make him grunt.

He released her with a smile, and she stumbled back from

him.

The king clapped him on the back. "Congratulations, Glenlyon."

Sorcha wiped her mouth with the back of her hand, her eyes glaring daggers into his.

Malcolm looked back at the king. "Thank you," he said, unable to keep the sarcasm from his voice.

Luckily, Charles was in a good mood. "You'll mean that one day, my friend."

Malcolm's eyebrow rose and Charles mirrored the expression.

"If this is how you reward yer friends, I'd hate to be yer enemy, sire," Malcolm said, giving the king a half-smile so he knew he was in jest. Partially.

Charles laughed. "I have rewarded you indeed. You are merely too stubborn to realize it." He nodded in the direction of Malcolm's new wife. "I've given you a wife who is not only fresh and young and beautiful, but she comes from fertile stock and is wealthy as well. Most men would be groveling at my feet for such bounty."

"Aye, well, I am not most men, sire."

Charles laughed again. "That is probably the most truthful statement you have ever uttered. Come. We will have a banquet and celebrate. Because whether you wish to believe it or not, I have indeed shown you great favor today."

Malcolm glanced back to his wife only to find her watching him. Their gazes met. And held. For a moment, a cursed flash of longing rolled around inside him, that he'd met a woman he could love with all his heart, or at least trust not to murder him in his sleep, and that he could take home and set to work on raising a dozen children. It had been a long time since he'd felt the softness of a woman beneath him. Felt any touch more gentle than the sharp burn of a blade. Weariness washed through him, and he shook his head. There would be no gentleness from the likes of her.

Instead, he was bound to the spawn of his enemy and the only home he had to bring her to was one that had been nearly destroyed in the skirmishes with her family.

Her father came to her side and took her arm, giving Malcolm a look that would have dropped him where he stood, if expressions had such power. He couldn't say he blamed the man. But that didn't mean he would let it stand. Malcolm let his gaze roam over his bride, letting a small smile play on his lips. One that grew as Campbell's face turned a red as deep as Malcolm's hair.

Malcolm may not have wanted the marriage, and his new bride had certainly demonstrated her feelings on the matter. But that didn't mean it wasn't without its advantages. While Malcolm promised no harm would come to the lass, he most certainly had not promised that he'd never touch her. Quite the opposite, in fact. He'd been commanded under no uncertain terms by the king to consummate the marriage. Oh, he had no intention of actually going through with it—that would mean he'd be shackled to her forever—but Campbell didn't need to know that.

Malcolm licked his lips, his eyes feasting on her. Sorcha paled, but she didn't cower. She straightened her back, her gaze meeting his. And then her gaze dropped, roaming over his form with an expression as lecherous as the one he'd used on her.

He chuckled softly. Oh, she was a spitfire, this one. His simple plan to extract himself from his marriage might not be so simple after all. For while his bride may not wish to be wed to him any more than he to her, he doubted very much she'd appreciate taking the blame for their failed nuptials. No help for it though. He would have to ensure his presence was so abhorrent she had no choice but to run from him.

And the sooner the better.

Chapter Five

Sorcha tossed back the remaining wine in her glass, wishing it were something stronger. Getting good and sloshed sounded completely wonderful at that moment. She needed to keep her wits about her, though. Malcolm MacGregor had already proven a worthy adversary. She had no doubt he loathed her as much as she detested him. Yet by all appearances, he was well pleased with their marriage.

He'd laughed and jested and accepted congratulations from half the court throughout the night while Sorcha had sat silent, her brain still refusing to accept she was now married. To a MacGregor.

Well, aside from his name, he might not be quite so bad. Those kisses in the alcove the night before had certainly awakened something in her. And he was quite handsome, now that she could see his whole face. He had an air of perilous intrigue to him that some women might find alluring. Though the man practically screamed danger. He was nothing like the refined lords and gentleman with whom she generally kept company.

She wasn't the only woman taking notice of him. Most of the ladies in the hall were stealing glances. Though, while they all seemed fascinated, none were bold enough to do more than stare and whisper behind the safety of their fans. There was certainly enough to fascinate. The laird was the stuff of many a dream. The green brocade of his coat covered broad shoulders and arms that looked as though they'd shred the material of his clothing, if he made any sudden movements. His long coat and vest hid the contours of his waist and buttocks, but his calves were on full display encased in their silk stockings. He already towered above most of the men, and the small heel on his shoe made his height even more impressive.

She'd imagined such a warrior's arms about her many times. So unlike the foppish men who seemed to abound at court. Dreamed of being whisked away from all the political intrigue and skirmishes that seemed to rule her father's house.

But the man she'd imagined hadn't been one who ruled his lands with an iron fist. Who gave no thought or care to those he harmed in his quest for revenge on his rival clan. He didn't have cold, hard eyes that stalked her every movement. Her dream warrior was large and imposing, certainly. But noble of bearing and manners.

Her new husband, a word she could scarcely put to the man at her side, did have a certain sort of noble bearing about him. Not of a courtly lord but more of a fierce king, arrogant, and commanding, brutish in size and manner. She struggled to reconcile the man beside her with the one who had laughed with her and kissed her breathless in the alcove.

He grabbed a hunk of meat from the table, and she blanched when he crammed it in his mouth. His laughter bellowed through the hall, though there was a hollow note to it that made her think he wasn't enjoying himself as much as he wanted everyone to believe. Juices from the meat ran down his chin and he absentmindedly wiped them off with the back of his hand and let out a mighty belch.

The lady seated beside Sorcha leaned over to her. "My Lord Glenlyon certainly is…vigorous." The woman took a dainty sip of wine, watching with fascinated disgust as Malcolm emptied his own tankard and grabbed the pitcher of wine from a passing page, sloshing it on the floor as he did so.

Sorcha frowned at him as a bit of the liquid splashed on the hem of her gown. "Vigorous is one word for it," she muttered in reply.

Malcolm turned to her. "Ken a few others, do ye?"

With another man, she might have been embarrassed to have been caught saying something unflattering. With this one? She smiled. "Oh, I can think of a few others more fitting. Piggish. Slovenly. Beastly."

His eyebrow raised. "Is that all?"

"No. But the rest are not fit for a lady to say."

Malcolm roared with laughter, genuine this time, and Sorcha was hard-pressed to keep a smile from her own lips. She buried her face in her cup until the urge passed.

Malcolm drained the rest of his wine and let out another robust belch. Sorcha grimaced.

"Must you behave so?" she hissed at him. "Surely if the king were here you'd behave in a manner more fitting of your station."

"Do ye think so?" he asked, clearly amused.

She let out a long-suffering sigh. "Perhaps not. You are a Scot, after all."

One who had been an outlaw most of his life, along with the rest of his clan, though she didn't dare say it.

"Dinna forget, lass. Ye share that blood through yer father."

"I'm certainly not likely to forget, since it's my Scottish blood that got me into this mess," she whispered to him. Then she sat back and gestured to the page behind her chair to refill her cup. "But my mother was English, and she saw to it that I was brought up to be fit company for polite society and a life at court."

Even when not with the court, they'd often remained in Edinburgh, instead of retreating farther north to the more wild estates of her father's land in the Highlands. She'd spent little time there, much to her father's dismay, though she didn't see the need to divulge that. And when her mother had passed away the year before, Sorcha had remained with her kin in London, visiting occasionally with her father, whenever he was in town.

"Surely ye expected to be married at some point," he said, throwing the bone he'd been gnawing on to the dogs that always scampered under foot.

"Of course, I did. But I'd hoped for…"

That eyebrow raised again and the heat crept back into her cheeks.

"Go ahead, lass. Out with it."

"Very well. I'd hoped for someone more genteel. An English lord. Or, at the very least, one of the more *civilized* Scottish nobleman who frequent court. Not some…some Highland beast who doesn't seem to know or care how a proper gentleman should act."

He stared at her, and for a moment, she thought she might have wounded his feelings. Then he shrugged. "Ye're not exactly what I'd hoped for either."

The blunt jab stung, though it was no more than she'd said to him. She couldn't help but wonder what he *had* hoped for. But he didn't elaborate. She decided to be grateful and leave it alone.

Malcolm leaned over her and the woman next to her and ripped a leg off the roasted peacock that had been stuffed back into its own feathers, and devoured the meat in one bite.

She rolled her eyes and sat back in her chair, nursing another cup of wine.

She had to admit, despite his size and deplorable manners, his hard-muscled body moved with a feline grace. Like the lion which emblazoned the MacGregor clan crest. He deserved the nickname. He moved like a predator, always on alert. The physical resemblance was uncanny, with his red hair puffed slightly about his face and his tawny amber eyes that seemed to see everything. Unlike the other gentleman at court with their ringleted wigs, the Laird of Glenlyon's hair was simply tied back with a green ribbon that matched his coat. Sorcha wasn't sure if she was embarrassed for his lack of complete and proper court dress or if she admired him his courage to be different.

He turned those disconcerting eyes of his on her, and she forced herself not to shrink back.

"Ye've hardly eaten," he said, motioning at her plate.

"I've eaten enough, my lord." In truth, anxiety churned her stomach so violently she could scarcely force a morsel past her lips. She didn't have too much longer before she'd be marched up to a chamber and thrown in with the Lion at her side. All the bravado that had kept her going until that moment began to wane.

"You should eat. Ye'll need yer strength."

The men about them laughed, the ladies giggling delicately.

"I...cannot," she said, her voice nowhere near as strong as she'd intended.

Malcolm scowled. "I wasna referrin' to tonight," he grumbled, casting a dark look at their companions. Which only made them laugh harder. "Well, not only to tonight. We've a long journey ahead of us. We leave at first light."

"What?" Sorcha's stomach dropped to her toes. "So soon? But I can't possibly be prepared to leave so quickly. I thought to have a few days, at least, to…"

Malcolm waved away her complaints. "I've been away longer than I anticipated as it is. I must return as soon as possible. Yer maid has already been instructed to pack what belongings ye'll need for the journey. Anything not essential may follow later."

Momentarily struck speechless, Sorcha stared at her plate. The bits of roasted fowl and eel, of which she was normally fond, no longer seemed remotely appetizing. So soon? But that gave her no time in which to plot an escape should her plans for the night go awry. No time to say good-bye to anyone, or even pack all her belongings. It was too soon. She couldn't possibly…

"I meant what I said, lass. The trip is long and not particularly comfortable. Ye are far too pale and underfed. I'm beginning to have serious doubts ye'll survive the trip, let alone life in the Highlands." He sneered. "I doubt ye have any Scottish blood left in you. Ye've been living too long at court."

Sorcha bristled. He wasn't wrong. Still, the idea that this uncivilized bastard of a man found her lacking in any way sent a surge of anger through her so strong she had to pinch her thigh beneath the table to keep from stabbing him with her fork. Perhaps she should, just to introduce the man to the utensil as he didn't seem to know what to do with one. While the rest of the court neatly cut their food with a knife and the fork Queen Catherine had made so popular, and placed proper, bite-sized pieces into their mouths, Malcolm continued to eschew the cutlery all together in favor of his hands.

"Forget the journey, my lord. You still have the night to get through!"

Sorcha glared at the man who'd called it out, which only made the group laugh harder.

"Aye, that's true enough," Malcolm said, glancing back

at her with renewed interest. "And with the way ye've been guzzling that wine all night, it'll be a wonder if ye can make it out of the hall, let alone into my bed."

Sorcha's mouth dropped open, and he leaned forward to take her hand. "People might assume ye're afraid to be alone with me."

She tried to tug her hand from his but he held tight. She forced a smile. "It has nothing to do with fear, my lord. I simply cannot stomach the sight of you."

His eyes flared for a second and his grip tightened again. He leaned closer, as if he were whispering lover's nonsense in her ear. "The feeling is entirely mutual, madam, I assure you. However, since I ha' no choice in the matter"—he kissed her hand, sat back, and spoke loud enough so the others could hear him—"I have no intention of forgoing the bounty set before me."

His eyes roved over her again, and she knew he wasn't talking about the meal she was ignoring. A shiver ran down her spine. It was a strange sensation, not entirely unpleasant. Though it certainly should be. She pulled on her hand as hard as she could and he released her.

"Eat, madam," he ordered again. "Ye'll need yer strength."

She had no desire to follow any order of his, but he was right in one thing. If she was going to hold on to her wits and escape from the brute she'd been given to, she would need her strength. She had no intention of letting him best her, in any matter.

She turned to her plate, suddenly ravenous, and ate everything put before her. With the rich meal settling in her stomach, the slight haze in her mind cleared. If her new husband thought her a poor match, she would delight in proving him wrong.

• • •

Malcolm watched his new wife push her food around on her plate, the full, plump lips he'd admired pinched in a narrow thin line. His plan was going perfectly. He had the court convinced he was happy, or at the very least, compliant with his marriage, and his bride was behaving as he expected. As a woman who'd been forced into a marriage with a man she loathed. When he stormed from their bridal chamber demanding an annulment due to the woman's insufferable nature, possible insanity, and certain refusal to consummate the marriage, the blame would be laid firmly at her feet.

Oh, he had no doubt the king would be angry and even try and insist they give it more than one day. But Malcolm would be perfectly within his rights to be granted an annulment no matter how difficult one might be to actually obtain. He should have someone look into their bloodlines. Perhaps a kinship could be found.

If none of that worked…well, Malcolm would have to try a bit harder to drive the poor woman away. An easy task, if her behavior was anything to go by. She looked like she was about to bolt from the room. Perhaps he could make her do just that and have the whole matter decided before the bedding ceremony ever occurred.

The musicians struck up a lively tune and Malcolm shoved back from the table, holding his hand out to his bride. "Come, wife! Let us dance."

Her mouth dropped open. "I thought you wished me to eat, my lord," she said, her eyes darting around at the jovial company surrounding them.

"So I do. However, since ye seem more inclined to chase yer food 'round the plate than actually put anything in that delectable mouth, I have a mind to help ye work up an appetite. Unless ye're feeling ill. Ye *are* rather pale. Perhaps ye dinna have the constitution for such vigorous exercise."

"That doesn't bode well for tonight, eh Glenlyon?"

someone shouted, to the delight of the rest of the assembly.

She glanced around again. Her hand tightened briefly on her knife, then she squared her shoulders and placed her hands in his.

"On the contrary, my lord, I've never felt better." She slipped her hand into his and for a moment the silky smoothness of her skin gliding across his made him forget the game he played. Her next words snapped him back.

"I just find the company I'm forced to keep disagreeable." She'd leaned in and whispered it for his ears only.

He returned the favor. "I couldna agree more, madam. But the music is lively, I'm full of good food and better liquor, and I'm in sore need of a diversion from this travesty of a celebration. So, dance we shall."

He pulled her into the area that had been cleared between the tables and swung her into the dance. He never missed an opportunity to let his hands linger. Where the other dancers let their hands graze, he entwined their fingers. If they were to hold hands, he brought hers to his lips and pressed a kiss upon them. When he lifted her—far more easily than he should have, the woman was too light by half—he kept her in the air a moment longer than the dance allowed. He brought her down slowly, his hands at her waist, his gaze burning into hers until she blushed and looked away. And during the moments the dance separated them, he kept his attention riveted to her until she squirmed with discomfort.

If at any point she'd exhibited any distress at his attentions, he might have felt some regret. It wouldn't have stopped him. He needed out of this marriage and he needed his wife to be the one to bolt. But he might have regretted her feelings on the matter. However, while her flaming cheeks and blazing eyes suggested she wasn't enjoying his actions, every disagreeable measure he tried only seemed to spur her on, rather than send her running.

She would be a tougher nut to crack than he'd anticipated.

In one thing he'd succeeded, though. He had the court convinced he'd accepted his marriage and couldn't wait to make it legally binding. He doubted anyone would believe if she claimed he refused her bed. Now, he needed to ensure she'd refuse his, and he could return home unencumbered. And disgrace the Campbells all in one shot. This journey might end in success after all.

The music ended, and he grabbed Sorcha about the waist and hauled her to him. She pressed her hands to his chest, holding him back as best she could.

"What are you doing?"

"Kissing my bride," he said, leering down at her until she flinched away. A minor qualm stole through him at the necessity for such tactics, but the woman had proved more stoic than he'd hoped.

Before she could protest again, Malcolm descended, capturing her lips with his. She struggled against him for a moment and then ceased. He almost stopped kissing her to see what she was up to. Instead, those soft lips of hers moved under his, returning his kiss, and an entirely different sort of heat burned through him.

He angled his head to deepen the kiss, and she opened to him. She tasted like spicy, sweet wine and her tentative response had his head swimming. He pulled her closer with a growl. She trembled in his arms but didn't push away. To the contrary, her hands came up to rest upon his arms and then hesitantly moved upward until she grasped his shoulders.

Forget the rest of the celebration. There was a chamber with a freshly made bed awaiting them. He nearly bent to scoop her into his arms when he froze. What was he thinking? He should not be enjoying this so much.

He stopped abruptly and set her away from him. She looked up at him, mouth slightly swollen from his kiss, eyes glazed with the passion they'd awakened. This was wrong. And completely against his plan. She needed to hate him, be willing to do anything, go along with anything, if it meant getting away from him.

He gazed into her eyes. Then raised his arm and wiped his mouth with the back of his hand just as she'd done at their wedding. A maid scuttled by with a tray of sweetmeats and he plucked the tray neatly from her hands, hauled her to him for a crushing kiss, and then carried the tray off with a laugh. Being sure to pinch the fine, plump arses of at least three more maids on the way back to the table. He left Sorcha standing alone on the dance floor, staring after him.

His companions clapped him on the shoulder, raised their glasses to him, made jest after jest until he thought he would go mad. Sorcha kept her distance for the rest of the evening. It was for the best. Yet the remorse he'd not wanted to feel crept in. He shouldn't have kissed her again. Though, if he'd wanted to accomplish making her hate him, it looked like he'd been a success. Each time her eyes found his through the crowd, the weight of her anger hit him full force. From a mere look.

She'd be magnificent in battle—with her dark hair and flashing blue eyes, her pale face blazing with righteous indignation. It would be worth the consequences of riling her anger just to watch her in action.

For the first time, Malcolm wondered if he would win this crusade. Or if he wanted to.

But he didn't have a choice. Bringing home a Campbell bride would be tantamount to introducing a poisonous viper into his clan's midst. He'd not endanger them. Not for a truce. Or his king. Or even for his own obviously misguided desires.

He needed Sorcha Campbell out of his life. For good.

Chapter Six

Sorcha stared at the large, empty bed and squeezed her fists to keep them from trembling. In a few moments, she'd be expected to climb into that soft nest of doom to consummate her marriage. An hour ago, that had seemed like a terrifying prospect. Now…she wasn't so certain.

When the great, hulking brute she'd had the misfortune of being forced to marry had dared to kiss her, her first instinct had been to drive her knife into the manhood of which he seemed so fond. But that had lasted only a moment. Then the heat that she had felt the night before ignited—the tingling sensation that had spread from her lips straight through to her very core.

She'd meant to shove him away, tear her lips from his. Instead, she'd found herself drawing him closer, opening to him. His kiss had been intoxicating, and not because of the whisky she'd tasted on his breath. That man was her enemy. He was a rutting, scarce-better-than-outlaw MacGregor, who had only married her under command from their king. She didn't know his reasons for kissing her. Perhaps he'd wanted to humiliate her. Wiping his mouth afterwards had been a nice touch, if that had been his intention. Though, as she'd done that at their ceremony, she couldn't lay all the blame for that one at his feet. Then again, she hadn't made her action so obvious while he'd made sure the entire court watched him.

Or maybe he was merely drunk and did what all drunk men do. Find the nearest woman to get a hold of and do whatever it was they wanted.

It shouldn't have been something she enjoyed. She shouldn't still be able to feel his lips upon hers. Her heart shouldn't still pound in her chest at the mere thought of him. Her traitorous body needed to be brought under control if she had a hope of emerging from their marriage unscathed. And still a virgin.

Because for a moment, she had imagined what it would be like if she did remain married to him. What it would be like to come back to this chamber and eagerly await her bridegroom.

Instead, she waited, trying to decide if she should run, hide, or fight.

The choice was easy. She was a Campbell. She would fight.

Thankfully, while the members of court would witness them climbing into bed together, they were not staying for the actual act. Which gave Sorcha her only chance to escape her impossible situation.

Berta pressed a vial into her hand. "A few drops from this and he'll be unable to perform no matter what his intentions. You'll wake tomorrow on sheets as white as the day they were sewn and yer husband none the wiser beside you. You'll be free of him."

"Are you sure this will work?"

"Absolutely. I used it myself on my Thomas a time or two when he was still alive, bless his soul. He'll wake with a slight headache, that he'll think was brought on by the whisky. Only a few drops, mind. Too strong and he might take violently ill.

Or worse."

Sorcha nodded her head. "I want him incapacitated. Not dead."

"Two or three drops. No more. Offer him a drink as soon as the witnesses clear out. You don't want to give him an opportunity to…take the matter in hand, before you can dose him."

Her maid winked at her, and Sorcha dropped the vial into the pocket of her plush robe.

"What if he will not drink?"

Berta stared at her hard and withdrew a small pen knife from her bodice. "If he'll not take the easy way out, defend yourself as you must." She went to the bed and slipped the blade beneath the pillow.

Sorcha shuddered and prayed such an act would not be necessary. Especially, as she wasn't all that confident such a tiny weapon would even scratch the surface of the warrior she'd married.

The commotion outside her door signaled the arrival of the court. And her husband. Sorcha tightened the sash about her waist, straightened her shoulders, and sucked in her stomach to try and keep her gut from revolting—because of what she meant to do and what might happen were she found out. And what might happen if she failed.

"Don't fret so," Berta said, pulling her in for a quick hug. "The laird made every indication to you and everyone else at attendance at the banquet that he relished the bedding ceremony."

Sorcha sighed. "That is true enough." His hands on her body while they'd danced had left very little to her imagination.

"Which plays well into our plan. As he is so obviously willing, his failure to consummate the marriage will be deemed a physical defect. It will, at least, give your family valid cause to protest the wedding. A delaying tactic, perhaps.

But one that could result in a dissolution of your contract. Especially, if he were sufficiently humiliated by his failure that he refuses to press his claim to you. Even the king can't argue with impotence."

"Yes, but if I fail to get the potion in his drink…or if he refuses the wine…"

She would be left alone in a room with a very large bed and a drunk Highlander who'd made no secret of the fact that he meant to use it, and her, well.

"Then use the knife."

Sorcha wasn't at all certain the potion would work, or if it did, that they'd gain the results they sought. How was she to get the drops in his cup without him seeing her? It was, however, preferable to attacking him with a blade, small as it was. She might still accidentally kill him. She'd spoken the truth to Berta. She didn't want the fiend dead, just gone. With her family unpunished. He died, and they'd be lucky to escape with their heads. Aside from the singular sin of murder, Glenlyon was a particular friend of the king's. She doubted His Majesty would look kindly on the one who finally did him in.

She took a deep breath. Two drops. Or three. And she'd be free.

Berta fluffed her loose hair about her shoulders once more, gave her cheeks a quick pinch to put some color in them. Then the door burst open, and in they marched. A pack of buffoons, led by the biggest one of all. He was already in his robe which gaped open at the waist, revealing a linen sleep shirt that left far too little to her imagination. The hint of muscle she'd felt through his clothes was nothing compared to the sight of them. There wasn't an ounce of softness on the man. He was solid rock from his calves to the top of his head.

Except for those lips. Full. Velvety. And that mane of hair on his head. Tendrils had escaped from the ribbon and stood about in a copper halo around his head. He almost looked angelic. If it weren't for those predator eyes.

"My wife!" he shouted, marching straight toward her and hauling her against him before she could utter a word of protest. He lifted her off her feet and kissed her soundly, to the delight of the onlookers who hooted with glee.

"My lord, please," she said, pushing against his chest, her feet kicking uselessly.

"Ah, hear that, lads? She begs for more!"

She gasped in outrage and renewed her struggle against him, little good though it did. He laughed, a great roaring bellow that rang through the chamber, and released her. She glared up at him, a dozen curses hovering on her lips. Her words were stayed with one glimpse into his eyes.

His mouth laughed. He responded to each ribald jest and comment with good-natured bawdiness. But the humor and joy never reached his eyes. They were cold and emotionless as ever. He wasn't enjoying this charade any more than she. She straightened to her full height and held his gaze. If he thought to intimidate her through his act, or prove that he was the most loyal with his willingness to fulfill the king's wishes, he'd severely underestimated her.

She motioned Berta over and held out her arms, allowing Berta to remove her robe. She wasted no time letting the men of court ogle her but marched straight to the bed and climbed in, pulling the covers up to her chin.

Malcolm's eyebrow raised, almost a salute to her challenge. "My bride is eager, my friends. Let's get this done so that we may be alone at last."

The men laughed, the women giggled, and Sorcha blushed five shades of flaming red. She risked a glance at her father and wished she hadn't looked. Her father's hand clenched repeatedly around his sword, his face growing more mottled with rage with every passing second. His anger strengthened her, calmed her nerves. She would show this rutting beast what it meant to be a Campbell. He thought to take her, make her his? He'd have a rude awakening come morning.

But first, she needed to get rid of the witnesses.

"It's growing late, my lord," she said, igniting another round of revelry that her husband ignored.

He looked at her, brow furrowed as he searched her face. Sorcha took care to keep her expression blank. Finally, he nodded.

"It is indeed." He turned to the crowd behind him. "My wife, it appears, is *verra* eager for my company."

He climbed into the bed beside her beneath the covers. He made no move to touch her, yet still, Sorcha did her best to remain stoic and not shrink from him.

One of the more inebriated lords lurched toward Sorcha. "I'll be happy to lend a hand, Lord Glenlyon. She looks to be too much for just one man to handle."

Several onlookers gasped, but most laughed, assuming the man's antics were due to an attempt at humor. But Sorcha shrank back from his grasping hands. She reached beneath her pillow, wincing when the blade pricked her palm. She needn't have bothered. Before she could bring the knife fully out, Malcolm nodded to the lord who'd been standing quietly in the corner, the one who'd flanked him after meeting the king. He immediately came forward and clamped a firm hand on the man's neck, hauling him away from Sorcha, and tossing him into the arms of his friends.

"I believe the requirements ha' been satisfied," Malcolm said, his face never losing its jovial grin though his voice was steadfast as steel. "It is time to beg a little privacy."

Sorcha balled the bedding in her fists, keeping her hands hidden so no one would see even the smallest indication of the panic that suddenly burst through her. She focused on taking slow, steady breaths and after a few moments was able to unclench her fist, the knot in her stomach slightly loosened.

"Ah, come on Glenlyon!" another voice said. "We must witness a kiss at least."

Malcolm went tense beside her, and Sorcha followed suit. He couldn't kiss her again. Not while they were in bed together. Not in front of witnesses! Her cheeks flamed so hotly her eyes watered and she blinked furiously to clear them lest anyone believe them to be tears.

Malcolm glanced at the king who laughed good-naturedly. "Perhaps a kiss would ease the troubled minds of your peers," he said. "A MacGregor and a Campbell, after all, is a volatile pairing. Come, my lord! Give your bride a kiss and we will leave you to the rest."

The crowd gathered around the bed laughed and cheered. Sorcha swallowed hard to keep her dinner from reemerging. She'd heard many tales of bedding ceremonies. Most of the time, the couple were put to bed and left in peace. But on occasion, there were instances where nervous families would insist on witnesses being present for the actual act, to ensure the consummation took place. Frankly, given their situation, Sorcha was a bit surprised the king hadn't demanded that very thing. Requiring a mere kiss was great fortune indeed. At least, considering the alternative.

She risked a glance at Malcolm. His expressionless face told her nothing of his thoughts or feelings. Then, he held his hand up with a smile that didn't reach his eyes. "Aye, gentlemen. And ladies. As ye wish," he said, impressively giving a gallant bow from his side of the bed. "One kiss, at Your Majesty's command," he said with a laugh that to Sorcha's ears, at least, sounded forced.

She had no time to steel herself, let alone protest. He was suddenly kissing her again. His lips moved over hers, hot and demanding. He pressed her back against the pillows as he plundered her mouth, drawing a moan from her lips despite her best efforts to remain unaffected.

He pulled away only briefly to motion everyone out, and then he was back, his lips moving over her jaw, and down her neck, raining hot kisses upon her until her head swam and she had to hold onto him just to anchor herself.

She was barely aware of the king taking a laughing leave while Malcolm's friend ushered everyone else out of the room. The door closed behind them, leaving her alone with her husband. Who still hadn't stopped kissing her.

She needed to stop this. Now. While she still could. While she still had any desire to do so. She reached beneath her pillow again and grabbed her dagger, whipping it out and pressing it against his throat before he had a chance to react.

He froze for a moment, staring at her with wide, surprised eyes. Then he laughed. A great, bellowing roar that rang throughout the chamber.

"Ye came prepared, did ye now? Aye, ye're a braw lass right enough. But," he said, capturing her wrist and plucking the dagger from it before she could make any other movements. "There's no need for that." He released her, tossed the blade onto the table by his side, and reclined back against the pillows with a deep sigh. "God's beard, what a night."

Sorcha jumped up and snatched her robe from where Berta had placed it near the bed. Her frantically beating heart calmed slightly when she reached her hand inside the pocket and felt the vial. It hadn't been discovered, or broken.

Malcolm glanced at her in surprise but said nothing as she moved away from the bed and toward a table where some wine, breads, and cheeses had been left for them.

She sloshed some wine into a glass and downed it to help steady her nerves.

Malcolm chuckled and swung out of bed, going to the fireplace. "That bad, is it, lass?" He kicked at a log on the hearth. "I suppose it is at that," he muttered. "If ye're inclined to share, pour me a glass, aye?"

He bent to stoke the fire and add more wood. Now was her moment. She poured them each half a glass. While she would have loved more, she needed to keep her wits about her. And she wasn't sure if she should pour him a bigger glass. That way if the poison failed, maybe a good old fashioned drunken stupor would take over. She didn't particularly care how he was incapacitated, merely that he was. However, too much wine and the potion might not prove effective enough.

She risked a glance over her shoulder. Malcolm was still busy with the fire. Her heart pounded so furiously she feared he'd hear. She quickly pulled the vial from her pocket, unstoppered it, and poured a few drops into one of the goblets.

Damn! Had that been three? Or Four? Possibly five? More than enough to do the job, at least. She quickly pocketed the vial again.

The clatter of the fire poker hitting the stone of the hearth startled her and she jumped, knocking over one of the wine glasses.

She grabbed a linen from the table and tried mopping it up, her hands shaking.

Malcolm's hand closed over hers and she froze. She sucked in one ragged breath after another, finally forcing herself to look up at him. He stared down at her, those amber eyes of his shuttered, confused. Like she was a puzzle he couldn't solve. He took the linen from her hand and finished cleaning up the spilled wine. Sorcha backed away from him, putting the chair by the hearth between them. She tried to position herself near the fire poker he'd dropped without making it too obvious what she was doing.

Malcolm glanced over and snorted. "If ye intend to use that thing on me, be sure to get a good grip on it first. It's heavier than it looks."

Embarrassment flooded her cheeks but she held her head

high. "I had no intention of doing such a thing."

"Aye, well maybe so and maybe no. But I figured I'd offer a word of advice, just in case."

She blew her breath out and plopped into the chair, though she kept her body rigid and ready to run at any moment. And she kept sight on the poker.

Malcolm never took his eyes off her but aside from a slight scowl, his face offered no hint of his thoughts. Finally, he sighed. "Ease yerself, lass. Ye have no need to fear me."

"I fear no one."

He nodded at the poker by her feet, silently pointing out the lie behind her words. "Be that as it may, I have no intention of forcing myself on you."

Sorcha frowned. "But…the way you acted, what you said…I am your wife now. We are supposed to…that is, I…"

Malcolm shook his head. "We may be wed, but I have no hold with rape. If ye'll not come to me willingly, I'll leave ye to yer peace."

"But…you're a MacGregor."

"Oh aye? And we're all rutting, murdering bastards, is that it?"

Sorcha couldn't tell if he was angry or merely annoyed. Or possibly amused. Either way, she felt it best not to worsen the situation by responding. When she didn't speak he snorted.

"Aye, well I guess ye've never been told any different. Though I can assure ye, lass, I've never touched a woman without her consent and I have no intention of doing so now."

His words calmed the turmoil raging inside her, at least a bit. Though she knew she shouldn't trust his word. "And what will the king say to that?"

Malcolm shrugged. "Perhaps we'll simply tell him we were too drunk to carry out the deed and beg his leave to be quit of each other." He gave her a little wink that surprised a laugh out of her.

"We are in quite a mess, aren't we?" she said.

"That we are, lass. That we are."

She looked down to fiddle with the hem of her robe and winced as the fabric brushed against the small cut on her palm from the dagger beneath her pillow. He was certainly not what she'd expected. Perhaps the way he had acted before the others was simply that, an act. For despite his earlier promises—threats, she should say—he didn't seem the least inclined to carry through with any of them. Maybe she didn't have anything to fear from him, after all.

"Is there a way out of it, do you think?" she asked him.

"There's always a way out of every situation. Unfortunately, I havena found a solution to this problem just yet."

Though he was echoing her own sentiments, a twinge of annoyance at being called a problem irked her. Still, he didn't seem inclined to attack her. That was a sight better than she'd expected. Perhaps he wasn't such a brute.

She heard the scrape of a goblet across the table top and looked up to see him raising his glass to her.

"To my wife. May she be so only briefly."

Sorcha laughed with him and then shot to her feet in horror. "No, wait!"

But he'd already drained the glass. But which glass was it? Had she spilled the one with the potion? Or had he drank it? All?

"What ails ye, lass?" he said. He took one step toward her and then lurched back against the table.

She had her answer. The expression on his face turned thunderous and even as incapacitated as he was, Sorcha took a step back and reached for the poker. She brandished it before her like a sword.

"Stay away from me," she warned.

Malcolm was too busy trying to stay upright to come for her. He put a hand to his head. "What did ye give me, ye treacherous witch? Did ye think to escape our marriage by murthering…murth…" He frowned and shook his head, staggering toward her.

He raised his finger, as if to scold her like some nursemaid admonishing her charge. Then his eyes rolled up in his head, and he crashed face first at her feet.

"Oh sweet Mother Mary, I've killed him." Sorcha dropped to her knees and tried to roll him over. The hulking brute wouldn't budge. His chest still rose and fell with regular breaths, so…that was good. She supposed. She prayed she was far away or there were ample witnesses when he awoke, or he was going to kill her.

Now, to stage the…her mouth dropped open in a groan and she stared down at the massive warrior at her feet. The one she couldn't even roll over. There was no way she'd be able to get him onto the bed. Having him face down on the floor sort of ruined the story that she'd been in bed, willing and waiting, and he'd been unable to perform.

She chewed at her lip for a moment, hands on her hips as she considered the new problem. If it was a problem. Her story was that, though he'd tried, he'd been unable to perform his husbandly duties to consummate the marriage. That didn't mean he needed to stay in the bed the entire night. In fact, having him passed out on the floor might work more to her favor. If he'd been upset over his failure and gotten stinking drunk, or better yet, chose to spend the night on the floor rather than sleep with his bride, that would help prove her point.

She turned and dragged a blanket off the bed and spent several minutes arranging him to look comfortable on the rug before the fire. Hopefully, the drug would wear off by morning. If she still couldn't wake him, it wouldn't help her story. And would go a considerable way to proving her own guilt.

Once he was neatly arranged to her satisfaction, Sorcha retrieved her dagger and climbed into the bed, pulling the remaining blanket over her. The dagger went back under her pillow. She should probably extinguish the candles, but she was too exhausted to get back out of bed. And, though she didn't like to admit it, she preferred to have the light, in case Malcolm woke in the night.

She'd like to see her death coming.

Chapter Seven

Malcolm cracked an eye open and groaned when the weak light from the window sent a beam of pain straight through his skull. He hadn't experienced such a nauseating pounding since he and John had been lads stealing his father's best whisky. He grunted when a small foot nudged him in the ribs but ignored it in favor of burying his head in his arms, trying in vain to protect his eyes from the light. The foot nudged harder.

He cracked his eye open again and peered up at a woman with a cloud of black hair framing her face. He squinted. And then he remembered. His wife. He was married now. Well, except for the small matter of consummation. Which hadn't happened because…what *had* happened?

He groaned and sat up, his hand supporting his aching head before it toppled off his shoulders.

"Oh good," she said, backing away from him. "For a minute there I thought you might be dead."

He snorted, though the sound sent another wave of pain crashing through his skull. "Dinna tell me you'd be upset to find yerself a widow so quickly."

"Not at all. But being charged with your death wouldn't make my situation any better either."

"Charged with my..." He frowned, and then the events of the past night came back with a vengeance. "Ye poisoned me!"

He lurched to his feet, and she stumbled back, holding her hand out to placate him. Slim chance of that. He'd have grabbed for her, but another pain thundered through his head and he grasped the ledge of the table to steady himself.

"I did not poison you," she said, though her face was an interesting shade of white. "I tried to stop you from drinking the wine but you didn't listen."

"Well, I didna know ye were trying to kill me. If ye'd warned me that you had laced the wine with something, I'd ha' listened better."

She snorted this time. "Doubtful. I haven't known you long, my lord, but you hardly seem the type to pay attention to any but yourself."

His head throbbed again and he slumped into the chair at the table, hand automatically reaching for the pitcher. He poured himself some wine and raised the glass to his lips. Just in time, he realized what he was about to do and hastily put the glass back down. Sorcha rolled her eyes.

"I didn't poison it."

He raised an eyebrow. "You'll understand if I dinna take ye at yer word."

"Oh, for heaven's sake," she said. Marching over to the table, she grabbed the glass he'd poured, took a healthy swallow, and placed it back before him. "There. You see. Perfectly safe."

He slowly reached for the glass, keeping his eyes on her at all times. She didn't make any sudden moves and seemed sound enough. He carefully took a drink, sighing as the cool liquid quenched his parched throat. It also dulled the roaring pain in his head and he sat back with a sigh.

"What exactly happened last night?" he asked.

She shrugged. "You were awake for most of it. After you…well, fell asleep…"

He raised his brow again, his lips almost twitching in amusement. The lass had audacity, he'd give her that. Poisoned him, bold as brass, and then had the temerity to stand before him and act as though nothing had happened. She'd definitely be one to keep his eye on. Not that he didn't already know that.

She glared at him but continued. "You fell asleep on the rug there and you were much too heavy for me to lift on my own, so I retired to the bed and slept until a few moments ago. Your man was pounding on the door and Berta, my maid, said that he is seeing to the preparations for your journey."

"So, after drugging me, ye decided to leave me on the cold floor rather than call for help?"

She shrugged again. "You were fine. Just asleep."

"Sorry to disappoint you."

Her scowl deepened. "I wasn't trying to kill you. If I had been, you'd be dead, make no mistake about it. But I wasn't going to let you come in here and ravish me, either. So I took a few precautions, that's all."

Malcolm frowned. "I wouldna ha' forced myself on ye, lass. I know I look the part of a raving beast, but that doesna mean I am one."

"Well, how was I to know that?" she asked, throwing her hands up. "My father tells me I'm to be wed to the man who has been our enemy all my life. A man who spends the evening showing me, and everyone else at court, how eager he is to get me into his bed. A man who, as my legal husband, has every right to do whatever it is he wishes to me. What else is a maid supposed to do?"

"So ye thought poisoning me would be a good way out?"

She released an exasperated sigh. "Of course not. Like I said. I wasn't trying to kill you. It was naught but a simple sleeping potion."

He rubbed at the ache between his eyes. "It was a bit stronger than a simple potion."

Her brow furrowed a bit. "Well, I might have given you a drop or two too many."

"Aye. That ye did."

She glared at him again but he ignored it. "And what, exactly, did ye think ye'd accomplish by rendering me senseless?"

Her cheeks pinkened and she spoke but wouldn't meet his eyes. "Our marriage remains unconsummated. And therefore, not completely legal, as of yet. As you were unable to perform your husbandly duties—"

"Unable because ye poisoned me."

She ignored that. "As I remain a maid, through no fault of my own—"

"Ha!"

She ignored that, too. "I intend to petition for an annullment."

Malcolm sighed and sat back in his chair, contemplating his bride. He didn't blame her for wanting an annullment. Hell, he'd had the same plan, although his hadn't involved poisoning his new spouse. But if she thought he'd let her disgrace him before the whole court, she was sadly mistaken.

"While I have no desire to remain wed to ye, I dinna think the king will entertain even the idea of an annulment, especially once the reason for my incapacity is known. In fact, madam, I'd be perfectly within my rights to have ye imprisoned for attempted murder. That seems a better solution to me than a simple annulment." He ran his hand over the stubble on his jaw, watching a growing wariness fill her eyes. "Aye. In fact, I should thank ye. You've provided me with the perfect solution to this predicament. You go to the Tower for attempted murder. And as your husband, I still retain the rights to your land and property." He nodded. "Verra neatly done."

Her jaw dropped. "You wouldn't!"

No. He probably wouldn't. Though it *was* the perfect solution. He'd be rid of her, yet still gain the advantages of being her husband without having to deal with her again. And after a time, no one would fault him for annuling the marriage. Unfortunately, while he could be an arse when the occasion called for it, he couldn't quite force himself to condemn a woman to a cell for the rest of her life. No matter how much she might deserve it.

She didn't need to know that, though. In fact, he might be safer if he kept that threat hanging over her head. At the very least, it might make her think twice before trying such a thing again. Either that, or it would inspire her to try harder the next time. If there had been any thought in his head that he and the woman he'd wed might find some way to make a marriage between them work, he was no longer under any such illusion. *Just as well.*

And, thanks to his resourceful wife, he now had the perfect excuse to annul their marriage. While he wouldn't be so cruel as to insist on her imprisonment, he would be sure to have a discreet word with the king and insist on an annulment on the grounds of the non-consummation of the marriage, due to his wife's heavy hand with the poison. Surely, the king wouldn't keep him wed to a would-be murderess. She could be sent to a nice, comfortable, and hopefully, far away convent, and he could return to his lands. Mayhap a might bit richer, if he could negotiate keeping at least a portion of her dowry. She had tried to kill him, after all. Or so it looked, in any case.

Before he could think on the matter too much more, a

knock sounded at their door. Sorcha drew her robe closer about her and went to admit whoever it was.

A flustered maid, Berta, Malcolm assumed, judging from the way the woman hurried to her mistress's side and began fussing with her, was followed by John, two other maids, the king's physician, and several other members of the court.

"What's all this?" Malcolm said, pushing to his feet. He ignored the throbbing in his head and glared at the sudden influx of people into his bedchamber.

"Nothing untoward, I assure you, Lord Glenlyon," Sir Robert Synder, the king's physician, said soothingly. "His Majesty simply wanted to be sure all was well with our newly wedded couple."

His gaze flickered over to where the two maids were busying themselves with the sheets on the bed. At a nod from one of them, he turned back to Malcolm with a benevolent grin. "Excellent. I will tell his Majesty."

John's eyes widened, and he gave Malcolm a considering, and impressed, glance. Malcolm scowled at him which only made his friend laugh.

"What?" Sorcha said, her face somehow simultaneously white and brilliant red. Much like the sheet that was being held up for inspection for everyone in the room. The snow white sheet with a small but distinct stain of scarlet red upon its surface.

While her consternation was somewhat amusing, Malcolm had to agree with her confusion. He knew for a fact, nothing had gone on in that bed the night before. At least not with him. While it was not beyond the realm of possibility that he had somehow managed to make love to his disagreeable wife, while in a severely intoxicated state, he was certain she would have mentioned the fact. Then again, perhaps she wouldn't. She wanted out of the marriage as badly as he and had been willing to poison him to prevent any consummation. Had it taken place, he believed she would do as much as she could to hide the fact.

Before either of them could say anything else, a commotion at the door announced the presence of His Majesty.

All protestations faded as everyone in the room bowed and curtsied. Charles looked about the room, a benevolent smile upon his face, obviously pleased with himself at a match well made. At least in his estimation.

The king glanced at Malcolm. "Good morning, Lord Glenlyon. And Lady Glenlyon," he said, giving Sorcha a gracious nod. "I see you spent a productive evening."

Sorcha marched to the bed. "I hate to be the bearer of bad tidings, Your Majesty, but…" She plunged her hand beneath the pillow but before she could withdraw it, Malcolm was by her side. He grabbed her wrist in a vice grip, squeezing so she could not grasp the knife he was sure was there. He pulled her upright and held her tightly to his side.

The king's eyebrow rose. "Is there a problem, my lord?"

Malcolm forced a laugh and held Sorcha tighter, wrapping his arms about her to keep her from squirming, though hopefully, it looked to the rest of the room that he was merely holding her in an affectionate embrace. "Naught but that a little rest might cure, Your Majesty. I'm afraid she's worn out from our wedding night and beside herself with all the scrutiny this mornin'. A lady's sensibilities being what they are, ye ken?"

"Of course, of course." The king graciously nodded and then beamed at the rest of the room. "Well, my friends, let us leave the happy couple to a few more hours of wedded bliss!"

There was much good-natured laughter and jests as the room cleared.

Sorcha began twisting in earnest. "Let me go!" She raised her foot and stomped on his as hard as she could. Malcolm grunted and released her. Not because it hurt particularly. But her writhing in his arms was causing a reaction he was sure she not only didn't intend but would be completely horrified by. He wasn't too pleased with his anatomy either. But it had a mind of its own when it came to half-naked women squirming against him.

John paused at the door, his look questioning. Malcolm sighed and waved him away. The grin on John's face left no doubt of the man's amusement at his cousin's expense. Malcolm couldn't be too angry. If their positions were reversed, he was fairly certain he'd be howling with laughter. Things weren't quite so funny on his end of the stick, though.

Only Sorcha's maid remained. She settled Sorcha into a chair and was fussing over her, pressing a wine glass into her hand, and generally carrying on as though the greatest calamity in all the world had occurred.

Malcolm fixed her with a stony gaze. "Out."

The woman stood her ground, hands on her ample hips and double chin in the air. "I'm here to care for my mistress. I'll not be ordered about by the likes of you, especially after the way you just treated her."

Malcolm stalked over to her until she had to crane her neck to look up at him.

"While your loyalty is commendable, your mistress is now my wife and I am under my full rights to treat her any way I see fit. If her servants canna obey my orders, then I'll find her more suitable people who know their place. Is that clear?"

Berta reluctantly nodded though hatred blazed from her eyes.

"Good," he said. "Now. Get. Out."

The maid looked as though she would argue again and despite the irritation flooding him at her insolence, Malcolm couldn't help a twinge of admiration. Grown men had cowered before him with half the cause. But brave or no, he had no intention of allowing an underling such freedom.

Sorcha stood and came to her maid, giving her a gentle pat on the arm. "It's all right, Berta. I'll call you when I need you."

The woman's eyes widened slightly but thankfully, she kept her disapproving mouth shut and turned on her heel.

The moment the door closed, Sorcha rounded on him. "What was the meaning of that?" she shouted, rubbing at her wrist again.

"The meaning of what?"

"What do you mean 'of what?' You grabbed me, nearly broke my arm, and prevented me from—"

"Are ye completely mad?" he asked through gritted teeth. He leaned toward the bed and flipped the pillow over, revealing the dagger she'd hidden there. "I prevented ye from being arrested for high treason. Drawing a blade in the king's presence would ha' condemned ye to death. Have ye no sense in that thick Campbell head of yours?"

She had the grace to blanch, realization finally dawning in her eyes at the crime she'd almost committed. "I had no intention of harming the king. Surely they would have realized that."

"Whether they would or no wouldna matter. They wouldna stop to ask yer intentions. And even if they had, the law is the law. To draw a blade in the king's presence is a hanging offense."

She blew an exasperated breath out and stomped away from the bed, looking for all the world as if she'd like nothing more than to plunge that gleaming dagger straight through his heart.

"I was merely trying to show the physician that the only blood that flowed from me last night was from that dagger pricking my hand, not…not…"

Malcolm snorted. "Not from *my* dagger pricking yer maidenhead?"

Sorcha glared at him. "Yes, damn you! Though you needn't be so crude about it. But since you kept me from doing so, the entire court thinks we are well and truly wedded and bedded and now I'm stuck with you!"

"Believe me, madam, I'm no' any more happy with the situation than you. Perhaps I should ha' let you pull the blade. Then at least I'd ha' been rid of ye."

"Oh!" she said, nearly spitting with fury. She grabbed a glass from the table and chucked it as hard as she could at his head. He neatly ducked and it crashed against the wall behind him instead.

"Try to refrain from destroying all my property, lass. Ye'll have me beggared within an hour."

"Your property? If we are wed now, then it belongs to me as well. Which means I shall do whatever I damn well please with it!"

Another glass sailed at him, and laughter built in his gut, despite his best efforts to remain angry. Still, best to excuse himself before everything he owned was destroyed. He quickly dressed while his new wife rampaged about the room.

"Madam," he said several times, trying to get her attention while she cursed at the burning logs she was viciously jabbing with the poker.

"Sorcha!" he finally yelled.

She stopped short and spun around with the poker in her hand, looking at him in astonishment. It was the first time, other than their marriage ceremony, that he'd used her Christian name.

He glanced at the poker she raised like a weapon and she blushed slightly while slowly lowering it. When he felt his life was no longer in imminent danger, he tried again.

"I must see to our preparations. I suggest ye stop acting like a spoilt child and pack whatever belongings ye need for the journey."

The hand holding the hairbrush she'd been about to throw dropped and her eyes widened. "What journey?"

He frowned, trying to decide if she was really so daft or if she merely enjoyed making him repeat himself. "Do ye not remember what I told ye last night? We travel for my home today."

"But…but I thought you were merely threatening that to upset me."

He had been, but that didn't change the fact that he needed to get home. Who knew what further trouble had occurred in his absence.

"'Tis true I'd hoped I wouldna have to bring ye along. But since ye saw fit to cut yerself on that damn dagger and make it appear for all the world like we well and truly bedded each other last night, we're stuck with each other for the now. While having ye along is inconvenient and unwelcome, ye are my wife and I dinna think the king would regard me kindly if I were to leave ye here, like to as I may. Since the only reason I agreed to this abomination in the first place was to appease him, it wouldna do me any favors to go against his wishes now."

Her face grew redder the more he spoke but he ignored the mild flashes of guilt that tried to plague him. He refused to coddle her. Since he'd not be able to get rid of her on the grounds of non-consummation, he was going to have to drive her away by acting like the beast she thought he was. And… he only spoke the truth.

"You needn't worry on that point," she finally managed to say. "If I must remain your wife, I see no reason why I must do so at your godforsaken estate. My parents very rarely lived under the same roof. I see no reason why we should."

"Because the king expects it and I'll no' be angering him, no matter what my feelings are on the matter. Besides, as ye have already pulled a blade on me and tried to poison me, leaving ye unattended to plot even more nefarious schemes against me wouldna be the best choice in the circumstances. Who knows what kind of mischief ye'd get up to, left to yer own devices? Or rather, those of yer murdering bastard of a father."

And it would be much easier to make her miserable enough to abandon their marriage, if he had her under his roof and watchful eyes. "While I'd like nothing more than to mount my horse and ride as far from ye as I can get, I'm no' going to let ye out of my sight. So," he said, ignoring the furious sputterings coming from his wife, "ye have two hours to pack what ye need, and *only* what ye need. We'll travel quickly, which means packin' light. The rest of yer belongings can be sent later. Someone will come for ye when it is time to go."

"I'm not going with you. You can't make me!" she shouted at him.

He ignored that. They both knew that he could.

"Two hours, madam. I suggest you use them wisely."

Chapter Eight

Sorcha stared at the door Malcolm had slammed in her face, fury rushing through her body so hotly her head swam. How dare he? What was she to do now?

A moment later, the door burst open and Berta bustled back in. "Oh, my lady. Are you all right?"

Sorcha waved her off. "I'm fine, Berta. Stop fretting." While grateful that someone cared for her welfare, it had been a taxing morning, and calming her maid's nerves was more than she could handle.

"That…that man told me I was to pack your belongings and have you ready to leave within the hour. He even berated me for not having you packed already, as he'd ordered last night. But why should I have done that when we'd no intention of accompanying that brute," she said, flouncing over to the armoire that held Sorcha's gowns.

Sorcha pointed to the one she wanted, a plainer gown with an overdress of brown silk, split to reveal an embroidered cream-colored panel. "I don't think we have a choice. Until I can find a way to rid myself of him, I must go where he bids."

"Oh, my lady," Berta muttered, deftly inserting her mistress into the gown. "Did he harm you last night?"

Sorcha blinked at her maid, not immediately understanding her meaning. Then it dawned on her that Berta believed what everyone else did. "No, of course not! I gave him the potion, and he spent the night drooling on the rug by the fire."

"Then…how…?"

"That damn dagger. I grabbed for it and pricked my hand and…" She sighed. "It's no matter now. What's done is done. Let's get my belongings packed before the bastard makes me leave everything behind."

Berta immediately bustled off, packing gowns, linens, and anything else she could get her hands on into Sorcha's trunks. Within the hour, Berta had pulled off the impossible and had eight trunks ready and waiting to go. She breathed a small sigh of relief. She might not have a choice about whether or not she had to follow her new husband into the highlands of Scotland, but at least she would not have to do so without her belongings.

When the door burst open a short time later and Malcolm strode in, Sorcha calmly stood to face him.

"What's this?" he asked, gesturing at the trunks and boxes strewn about them.

"My belongings," she said, frowning at him. "You said to have everything packed."

He shook his head, disbelief plain on his face. "I said to pack only what ye needed for the journey."

"This *is* what I need."

He cursed under his breath and pointed to Berta. "You. Pack only what she absolutely needs while we travel. If it doesna fit in that," he said pointing to one of the smallest boxes, "it doesna come."

Sorcha opened her mouth to argue but before she could,

he'd turned his attention to her, looking her up and down with an exasperated sigh. He reached behind him and the servant girl who'd been waiting thrust a wool gown into his hands and then scampered off.

"I had a feeling ye wouldna have appropriate travel clothing. Wear this. It will hold up to the rigors of the road a fair bit better than that frock ye have on."

She looked down at her dress. "What is wrong with this? Surely it will do well enough in a carriage…"

"Ye'll not be riding in a carriage. I told ye, we'll be traveling quickly, by horseback. The rest of these," he said, waving at her trunks, "can follow along later."

"But Berta doesn't ride…"

"Berta willna be accompanying ye."

Sorcha gasped, shock and outrage momentarily stealing her tongue.

"Probably for the best, anyway," he said, glaring at her maid.

"The best for whom?" Sorcha sputtered.

"For me, o' course. The last thing I need is someone fiercely loyal to the Campbells stirring up trouble. I'll have my hands full enough watching my back with you in my household."

Dread filled Sorcha. Dread and sadness. Berta had been with her as long as she could remember. She'd counted on her to be her eyes and ears, to help protect her. Now she'd be walking into the enemy's territory with no one to rely on but herself.

"It's unseemly," Berta protested. "My lady cannot travel on her own. And she'll need a maid once she arrives at her new home."

Malcolm frowned. "She can choose a new maid once she arrives in Glenlyon. And she willna be on her own. She'll be traveling with her husband and his men. I promise ye, we are far more capable of guarding her from the dangers of the road than you."

"Yes, but who will guard her from you?"

"Berta!" Sorcha said, both touched and scandalized that her maid would speak so to the Laird of Glenlyon. Malcolm would be well within his rights to exact any number of harsh punishments.

He glowered at her and stalked closer, speaking in a low, rumbling tone that was all the more ominous for its quietness. "As I am the one who ended up poisoned on the chamber floor on our wedding night, I trust I'm the one with the most reason to fear for my safety." His eyes flickered back to Sorcha. "I may not have wished this union, madam, but I have given my word to yer father that ye'll come to no harm under my care. Whatever you Campbells think of my clan, even you ha' never had cause to doubt the word of a MacGregor."

He marched back to the door and paused to give her one last look, his eyes roving over her from top to bottom with a burning heat that had nothing to do with anger. She shivered despite the effort she made to remain unaffected.

"Are you cold, my lady?" Berta asked, fetching her shawl.

Sorcha waved her off. "No, no, I'm…" She glanced up at Malcolm, whose small smile suggested he knew exactly how he affected her. "I'm quite all right," she said, straightening her back and raising her chin in the air. *Damn the man.*

"Dress warm." He winked at her and left the room before she could sputter out a response.

The door slammed behind him and Berta immediately launched into a tear-filled tirade that had Sorcha's head pounding. Sorcha would have liked nothing more than to join her, but she only had minutes to repack her box. And she feared that if she released the storm raging inside, she'd never be able to contain it.

Once her box was packed, she threw her cloak around her shoulders and pulled Berta into a fierce hug.

"Stop your fretting," she said, with one last squeeze. "You'll be along soon enough."

"Yes, but my lady, without me there you'll be all alone with that man. Amongst the enemy."

The thought did cause a pit to open in her gut but she put on a brave face for Berta. "Don't worry for me. I can handle him. I think I proved that well enough last night."

That drew a tremulous smile from her maid and Sorcha released her and quickly pulled on her gloves. "Besides, as much as I hate to praise any MacGregor for anything, he is right about his word. I do not think I'll come to harm, if he can prevent it. I, on the other hand, gave no such promise. He may still regret dragging me along with him."

Berta returned her mischievous smile and directed a page to carry Sorcha's box down to the party waiting in the courtyard below.

Oh, Sorcha might have had no choice about accompanying her husband into whatever godforsaken swampland he called his home, but there was no law saying she had to make it easy on anyone. In fact, she had every intention of making Malcolm rue the day he slipped that ring on her finger. She'd have him running back to the king in no time, begging to be released from their bond. She almost pitied him.

Almost.

. . .

Malcolm, John, and the few men they'd brought with them waited impatiently for Sorcha to make an appearance. John clapped his hands against the cold.

"Perhaps if ye sent a servant to see if she needs assistance?" he suggested.

Malcolm squashed the flare of irritation. He was fairly certain Sorcha was purposely making them wait, just to vex him. If that was her goal, she'd accomplished it admirably. None of that was John's fault, though, so Malcolm kept his thoughts to himself.

By the time she made an appearance, he was ready to storm the palace and haul her out kicking and screaming. And in case he had any doubt as to her feelings for him, instead of apologizing for keeping everyone waiting, she swept by him like a queen in a procession. Her maid followed close behind, pausing only to drop her mistress's box at his feet.

Malcolm risked a glance at John and wished he hadn't. His cousin was nearly beet red with barely contained laughter. Malcolm scowled, scooped up Sorcha's box, and added it to the pack horse. John gave him a raised brow. Malcolm grumbled under his breath but marched over to his bride to assist her onto her horse.

She barely glanced at him, turning instead to embrace her maid. After several minutes of tearful good-byes, Malcolm lost his tenuous hold on his patience.

"We must leave if we are to reach our destination before nightfall."

Sorcha gave her maid a final hug and then turned, lifting her foot so he could boost her onto her horse. She didn't even bother watching him expectantly. Just left that little foot dangling in the air for him to hoist. He snorted and wrapped his hands about her waist, lifting her easily. If he held her a little too closely and a bit longer than necessary, well, a man was only a man, after all, and for all her sputtering and protests, her eyes flared with the same heat his did every time they were within sight of each other.

"What do you think you're doing?" she asked, with all the regal disdain of a pampered queen rather than a Scottish half-breed wench whose feet were dangling in the air.

"I thought perhaps my wife required a bit of assistance. Did ye not?" He held her even closer and she gripped his shoulders to brace herself.

Her eyes darted to his lips and her own parted with a slight inhalation of air. In fact, her breaths seemed to be coming much quicker than a few moments ago and her cheeks were flushed a becoming shade of red. Her hands tightened on his shoulders ever so slightly, sliding up a bit so she was holding him back rather than holding on. All he had to do was lean forward to claim her mouth.

He stopped with an inner groan, closing his eyes briefly to shut out the tempting sight of her. What kind of sorceress was she that he forgot himself so completely whenever he touched her?

She still watched him. Expectant. That wouldn't do at all.

"Are ye having trouble breathing, lass?" he asked, unable to resist needling her.

It broke whatever spell being held against him had put her under.

Her mouth smiled at him while her eyes glared daggers. "Yes," she said, with a mock-friendly tone. "That tends to happen when one is being crushed to death by a savage, uncivilized brute."

Uncivilized, eh? "My apologies, madam." He hefted her to her saddle before she could blink again. If he did so a little too eagerly so that she landed more like a sack of flour than the gentle lady that she supposedly was, well, that hadn't been his intention, but madam might benefit from a bit of humbling.

"My apologies again, madam. It appears I dinna ken my own brutish strength."

She glared at him and righted herself on the horse, spreading her skirts out with a flick of her hand. Malcolm quietly chuckled and mounted his own steed.

His amusement quickly turned to wary irritation when Angus came ambling across the yard toward their group. He gave Malcolm a brief but scathing glance and then nodded at his daughter.

"Write when you arrive. Keep me abreast of your welfare."

Sorcha's eyes widened slightly in surprise but she nodded with a small, pleased smile.

"Of course, Father."

"Remember who you are," he said, though his eyes locked with Malcolm's.

"Perhaps *you* would do better to remember who she is," Malcolm said. He'd have probably done better to let the slight threat behind his words go, but letting Campbell get away with anything went against Malcolm's nature. He continued, drawing his horse closer to Sorcha's.

"She is now my wife. And a MacGregor."

Campbell's face darkened. "A piece of paper doesna change the blood that flows through her veins."

"Aye, that's true enough." Malcolm nodded at the old man. Sorcha might be his by marriage, but she'd always be her father's creature. Something he'd do well to remember.

"It's growing late," he said, turning to lead them out of the gates. "Take care ye dinna fall behind," he said to Sorcha.

Her father stood aside to let them pass and after one brief glance, she turned her attention forward. And didn't look back.

The woman might be a burden he had not wanted or needed, but she was a brave lass, he'd give her that. With her back straight and her head proud, she left all that she knew and cared for to travel with strangers to an unknown land far from her home.

Unfortunately, her magnanimous attitude only lasted until her father was out of sight. Then her shoulders slumped, along with her mood, which turned as sour as the puckered discontent on her face. After they had stopped for the third time in under an hour so one of his men could pad her saddle with yet another cloak to cushion her genteel backside,

Malcolm had had enough. Before he could unlease some frustration, John appeared in his eyeline, interrupting his view of his wife who was complaining loudly, despite several men standing about waiting to pamper her.

"I'm feeling a most urgent need to relieve myself," John declared.

Malcolm's eyebrow rose. "Thank ye for keeping me abreast of yer bodily needs, however I fail to see what ye're expecting me to do about it."

"I simply thought ye might benefit from a similar diversion. Come. The walk might do ye some good. Clear yer head." He paused and looked pointedly at Sorcha. "Give ye some time to gain control over yer mouth before it gets ye into trouble."

Malcolm glared at his cousin but the man had a point. If he were to unleash his frustration at his bride's childish delaying tactics in the midst of her fawning group of admirers, he'd probably end up dealing with a case of mutiny. His men respected him and followed him without hesitation, but Sorcha was young, vibrant, and beautiful. The battle would be over before it began.

Without a word, he turned and marched into the shrubbery along the roadside, leaving an amused John to follow behind.

Malcolm relieved himself, taking his time as he was in no hurry to return to his wife's side.

"I think the men and I should travel on ahead," John said, surprising Malcolm out of this foul mood.

"What?"

John shrugged. "Ye have just been wed, after all. The last thing ye need is to be sharing yer wife with half a dozen other men."

Malcolm snorted. "I dinna believe she wishes to be alone in my company."

"I wasna suggesting giving her a choice in the matter.

Ye're newly married. Ye need time to get to know each other. How else will you discover if ye're compatible or not?"

"I can tell ye that right now. We're not."

"Aye, but unless she's disturbed by it enough to leave ye and petition the king for an annulment, you're stuck with each other. Right now, she hasna had to suffer your presence, as she has an entire retinue of men catering to her every whim."

He nodded over toward the rest of the group and Malcolm wasn't sure if he was more irritated or amused at the way his wife had twisted his men about her little finger. They danced attendance on her, offering her sips of water from their drinking bags or bits of bread or cheese they had pocketed away.

"I'm surprised they aren't feeding her morsels from the palms of their hands."

Before he'd even finished speaking, one of his men broke off a crust of bread and held it up to Sorcha's lips. She leaned down with a grateful smile and daintily nibbled at it.

"Oh, for the love of all that's holy." He sighed heavily and looked to the skies. "Lord gi' me strength." He fought the sudden temptation to break off the hand of the man feeding her and turned his back on them. He knew she was doing nothing more than everything in her power to drive him mad... He sighed again. Damn her, it was working.

John snorted. "If ye're hoping the journey will make her want to turn tail and run back to her father, I'm afraid yer plan may be ruined before it's begun."

Malcolm frowned. "That wasna my plan."

At John's questioning smirk, his frown deepened. "Not really. I'm no' going to go out of my way to make the lass uncomfortable."

"Nay, but I dinna think ye'll be going out of yer way to coddle her either."

Malcolm allowed a small smile to peek out. "Not to be

mean-spirited, mind. But life in the Highlands willna be like what she's accustomed."

"Och, come now. It's no' like ye live in a sty with the pigs. Ye've a grand keep to bring yer bride home to."

"Aye, a grand keep with a crumbling roof, damp walls, and empty rooms. Just what a highborn lady always dreamed of."

John shrugged. "Dreams change."

"Not hers," Malcolm said, taking a deep breath. He couldn't wait to get back home. Despite his friendship with the king, or perhaps even because of it, he did not feel safe in England. Charles might trust him but most of his court did not. They viewed Scotsmen as they would a barely broken stallion. Useful, when the situation called for it, but not fit for polite society. Aye, Malcolm would be happy to see the rolling, heathered hills of his home again. Even with the Campbell vixen trailing behind him.

"Call the men over," he instructed John.

After giving the men their orders, Malcolm transferred the provisions he and Sorcha would need to his horse and mounted up. Sorcha bid the men good-bye with an angelic smile. The moment they turned the bend, she rounded on him.

"I find it hard to believe you are so enamored you couldn't wait to be alone with me. So would you please explain why you've decided to leave us unprotected and alone for the rest of the journey?"

Malcolm smiled. Here was the shrew he knew and would never love.

"Ye're hardly unprotected, madam. I'll protect ye from any harm, as I promised."

She snorted. "I didn't take you for a sentimental man."

"Sentiment has naught to do with it. 'Tis a matter of honor."

"Oh yes. Men and their honor. Fairly certain that honor is what put us in this mess in the first place. Your honor that requires you to attack my father, and his honor which demands he retaliate."

"I believe you have that order reversed. I've never attacked your father unprovoked."

Sorcha sighed. "We can argue that point until we are blue in the face but I don't have the patience for it at the moment. Suffice it to say, I've had my fill of men and their damnable honor. So…what is your true reasoning for insisting that we travel alone?"

"Perhaps I was merely jealous that my men were the focus of all your attention."

Sorcha laughed at that. "Doubtful, my lord."

"Och, ye misunderstood me. I dinna want my men's attention on anyone but me."

"Well that's…odd," Sorcha said, her brow furrowing.

"If they are busy catering to an overly pampered, spoiled brat, they willna be aware enough of their surroundings and any possible problems, to be of any help to me should danger arise."

Sorcha's face turned redder with each insult he hurled at her. He was only slightly sorry for it. After all, he did speak the truth.

She kicked her horse into a trot and started down the trail the men had taken. Malcolm spurred his horse after her. For a moment, he almost believed she'd keep silent. But, of course, she wouldn't let an insult like that pass her by.

"I'm not spoiled or overly pampered," she said, keeping her stony gaze ahead.

Malcolm chuckled. "Are ye not?"

"No."

"Ye said yerself, ye've lived most of yer life at court. Save for the years his Majesty was in exile. And even then, I'm certain ye never felt want. Never worried for a roof over yer head. And not just any roof, I'll wager. But a fine, gilded one large enough to shelter half a village of people. With servants to bring ye anything ye may desire."

"You know nothing about me or my life."

"I ken enough."

"After one day?"

"Ye're a Campbell and yer father's daughter. That's more than enough."

"How nice for you to be able to judge a person based solely on their name."

"No more than ye've done for me."

He could almost feel the anger coming off her. He doubted very much anyone had ever spoken to her so. It was definitely past time for that to change.

"Perhaps we shouldn't speak," she suggested.

"Ye'll hear no objection from me." Though he seriously doubted she'd be able to maintain her stony silence for the rest of the day.

She surprised him.

She not only did not speak, she didn't acknowledge by any look or mannerism that she was even aware of his existence. After a few hours, he turned his horse off the road into a small glen. The upside to her refusal to speak was that he hadn't had to listen to her complaints. But whether she wanted to admit it or not, she was so tired she was slumping in her saddle. It was time for a break. He didn't want the trip to be comfortable for her necessarily, but he wasn't trying to kill the lass either.

She followed when he left the road but stopped her horse several yards away from his and dismounted without his help. He wasn't sure how she did it, but she almost made it seem as though she'd decided to take a break of her own volition. She neither looked at nor spoke to him while she stretched her muscles with a soft groan.

Malcolm ignored the slight twinge of guilt the sight sparked. She'd need to toughen up a bit. He loved his home, but it was no palace. Sorcha would be expected to pitch in and help, as everyone else did. He had no doubt she'd been trained since birth to manage a large household, but somehow, he didn't think a crumbling manse in the middle of nowhere was what she'd had in mind.

He walked over and held out a water skin. She didn't take it. In fact, she didn't even acknowledge he stood before her.

"Ye must be thirsty, lass. Take the skin."

She reached down to shake out the hem of her dress and pretended to adjust her shoe. Malcolm snorted. "If that's the way ye want it." He left the skin on the ground by her feet and went back to his horse to take out a small bundle of food. Normally, he'd have let her have first choice from the crusty bread that had been baked that morning and the bits of meat and cheese he'd obtained from the kitchen. But since she wanted to be childish about it…

He wrapped up a portion for her in a handkerchief and tossed it in her direction. It bounced off her chest and landed in her lap. She gasped with surprise and annoyance.

"Food," he said through a mouth full of bread, gesturing to the bundle. "Enjoy it while ye can. From here on out it's travel rations and whatever I manage to find along the road. No need to be worrit, though. There's always a few rabbits about."

Her eyes flickered to him briefly before turning back to her makeshift meal.

He didn't let them rest too long. He wanted to make their destination by nightfall, a small inn that he had stayed at before. There wouldn't always be such places and when there weren't, they'd sleep beneath the stars. But he would certainly take advantage of the shelter when they could.

After he'd packed up the remains of their meal, he glanced over to see Sorcha looking around, presumably for a rock or tree stump that would enable her to mount her horse without his help. Unfortunately for her, there weren't any suitable items lying about. And it would deprive him of the opportunity to ruffle her feathers a bit more.

He came up behind her and put his hands on her waist. She gasped and spun around, pressing back against her horse like he was going to attack her.

"I'm only going to help ye mount," he said, unable to keep the amused grin from his face.

"I can do it perfectly well on my own, thank you."

"Are ye so afraid of me touchin' ye, then?"

Her cheeks flushed redder than the hair on his head and he chuckled.

She glared at him. "Of course not!" Still, she stepped back away from him.

He stood back and folded his arms. "All right then. Go ahead."

She glared at him. He smiled back. He'd seen experienced horsewomen have difficulty mounting without help. It took some talent to navigate one's voluminous skirts onto the back of a horse taller than the rider. Even with the toned down, sturdier traveling garment he'd obtained for her.

Her glare melted into a sickly sweet smile he didn't trust for an instant. Keeping her gaze locked with his, she stooped over, gathered her skirts in one arm, hiking them nearly to her thighs, and with the other hand firmly on the saddle pommel, she hauled herself up and into the saddle. A few twitches of her skirts, and she was demurely covered and properly seated on the side saddle.

Malcolm blinked. He'd just seen more of her than he'd seen even the night before when she'd been clad only in her chemise. The glimpse of firm legs and shapely calves had him wondering what other heavenly bits she had beneath those skirts of hers. His imagination had him picturing it all too well.

"Is there a problem?" she asked, the smug tone of her

voice letting him know she was very aware of the effect she had on him.

He scowled. "Aye. We're still several hours from our stop for the night, and we are running out of daylight."

"Well, then. Stop standing around gawking and let's get going."

Malcolm muttered to himself under his breath and guided his horse back onto the road. "Keep up."

"Don't you worry about me."

He snorted. "It's me I'm worrit about," he murmured, too low for her to hear.

The last thing he needed to feel about his wife was more confusion. His body was in a constant state of war between wanting to kiss her or do deadly battle. Neither would be good, and thinking about both was exhausting. And he had another two weeks alone on the road with her.

He sighed and rubbed his chest, fairly certain an acute case of indigestion was imminent. Two whole weeks.

He'd never survive.

Chapter Nine

Sorcha stared at the bed they'd been given in the inn, her hands on her hips and a frown growing deeper by the minute.

"Where are you going to sleep?" she asked Malcolm, dreading the answer.

His eyebrow rose. "In the bed."

She rounded on him. "Absolutely not. I refuse to share a bed with you."

"Excellent," he said with a grin. He tossed a pillow at her. "I'm sure ye'll be verra comfortable on the floor. Or perhaps in one of the chairs by the fire."

Sorcha sputtered in indignation, both shocked and dismayed that he'd taken her up on her bluff. "You can't mean that. I'm a lady…"

"Aye, and I'm your husband. It's all perfectly acceptable. And even if that werena true, I wouldna care and neither would anyone else. I'm weary. We have a very long journey ahead of us, and it's already been a tiring day. I'm going to sleep. Ye can do what ye wish."

Sorcha watched as he finished removing his boots and

then unwound his plaid from his body, leaving him only in the voluminous white shirt that hung nearly to his knees. Her mouth grew dry, and she tried to lick her lips as she stared at him. She'd never seen a man wholly naked before, and she had the sudden urge to whip his shirt off and get a good look. But he might take that the wrong way, and the last thing she wanted to do was make him think she was interested in him as anything other than a means to an end.

He lay back against the pillows with a soft groan and flung his arm over his face. "Sorcha, come to bed. We managed to be in the same bed together last night without any dire mishap. Well, unless ye're counting the poisoning, of course."

"I told you that was an accident."

"If ye say so, lass. In any case, I promise I willna ravish ye or force any unwanted advances on you while ye're in this bed. My only desire at this precise time is to sleep. So come to bed."

She continued to stare at him, not sure what she should do. Of course, he had promised not to cause her any harm, and forcing himself on her would certainly be doing that. Though, he was completely within his rights as her husband to do whatever he wished to her. So why should she make it easier on him. Then again, though it was probably the dumbest thing she'd ever done, she trusted him. Oh, he did his level best to get on her nerves. He was insulting, rude, aggravating, and sometimes downright antagonistic, but for the few moments they'd shared the bed the night before, he hadn't made any advances she would consider threatening. Or even inappropriate. Well, after the kissing, of course.

She sighed and rubbed a hand over her face. If she were truly honest, she didn't really care. Fatigue had seeped into her very bones until she was ready to fall asleep where she stood.

"Fine," she mumbled. "Just…stay on your side."

"Wouldna dream of venturing into enemy territory, my dear wife. Rest assured, ye are safe from any unwanted advances."

So he said. But just in case... She grabbed the pillow Malcolm had left for her use and placed it between them in the bed. Not that something so flimsy would stop him were he to change his mind, but it did make her feel marginally better.

Malcolm cracked open an eye, gave a faint rumbling snort, and turned over on his side.

Well, she might have to crawl into the bed with him, but she wasn't going to do it half naked. Besides, without her maid, getting to all her laces was a bit of an issue. She climbed into the bed fully clothed, removing only her shoes, and carefully lay back on the pillow. Her body nearly cheered with relief. She resisted the urge to snuggle down into the mattress and lay stiffly on her side, her back to her husband.

She sighed. Definitely not the way she envisioned spending her honeymoon. She'd thought to spend the time entwined in the sheets, not using them as a barrier to keep the rutting bastard away from her. Not that he seemed too inclined to push the issue. She squashed the rush of indignation that manifested at the thought. She didn't *want* him to desire her. That would only make matters more difficult. Still, it stung her pride a little that he didn't even try to claim his husbandly rights. Aside from a few heated glances that she might or might not have imagined, he'd shown nothing but irritation at her presence.

She shifted uncomfortably, and the lump next to her sighed.

"Ye'll never get comfortable enough to sleep fully clothed. Do ye need help undressing?"

"No!" she said, slapping a hand to her chest and shifting farther from their makeshift barrier.

"Och, keep your mock modesty to yourself, lass. I wasna

trying to trick ye into giving away yer virtue."

"Why not?" The question was out before she could stop it.

Malcolm snorted.

"I meant to say," she swiftly added, "it seems most men would try to take advantage of the situation. It's not that I want...that, mind you. But...well, most men..."

"Aye, well I'm not most men."

"I've noticed," she mumbled.

He sighed and rubbed a hand over his face. "Look lass, I've told ye before. I've no interest in rape. Ye're bonnie enough, but ye're pricklier than a boar with a thorn in its hind end—and a Campbell on top of it. Ye're not exactly what I had in mind as a wife."

The words hurt more than they should. She didn't want him but she wanted him to want her. She had her pride.

"Really? And what exactly does a man like you want in a wife? Someone who can ride at your side when you raid villages, steal cattle, and hurt innocent people?"

He surged up so quickly she gasped, fear pumping through her blood.

"Listen closely," he said, forcing his words through gritted teeth. "I've told ye this before and I dinna like to repeat myself, so mark my words well this time. I've never hurt an innocent soul, and I've never stolen anything that didna belong to me first. I've never ridden against any clan that didn't attack me and mine. I canna fault ye for your blood, nor for what ye've been taught probably since your birth. But I'll no' listen to the lies your father has filled yer head with.

"And aye, I'd hoped to someday find a wife who could ride by my side. Who could help me care for my tenants and my land. Who would give me bairns and bring some comfort and peace into my life. But instead of peace..."

"You got me," she said, her voice so low she could barely

hear it and doubted he could. His words haunted her. He either spoke the truth or was a very skilled liar. She knew which her father would say. And while Malcolm's words had the ring of honesty to them, how could she believe him over her own father? Malcolm was the one who had every reason to lie.

She stamped down the sympathy that threatened to rise and hardened her heart against him again. He wasn't to be trusted.

"You weren't what I had hoped for either," she said, her voice soft in the darkness.

"I ken that, lass. And I'm sorry for it."

"That won't get us out of this mess."

"Say the word, lass, and I'll take ye back to your father."

Sorcha laughed mirthlessly. "A Campbell never concedes defeat."

"Neither does a MacGregor."

"Well then…"

"Aye. We're good and stuck, it would seem."

"So it would seem."

Malcolm sighed and laid down, staring at the ceiling with one arm tucked behind his head.

"Go to sleep, lass. We've got a long journey ahead of us."

She turned back on her side without another word. There was nothing else to say. It was in an impossible situation with an impossible man. Who, unfortunately, seemed just as stubborn as she. If there was any hope of driving him away, she was going to have to make her presence in his life truly unbearable.

She smiled into the darkness. This might actually be fun.

• • •

Almost a fortnight later, Malcolm was at his wit's end and

they still had a day left of their journey. Two, if Sorcha continued her maddening displays of ineptitude. Gone was the competent, if a bit spoiled, young lady he'd married. After that first night, she'd become a bumbling, complaining, crying mess of a woman. It took every ounce of patience he had not to leave her on the side of the road or put her over his knee and spank some sense into her.

Every new day seemed to unleash a fresh new hell. Today, she'd been talking incessantly since daybreak. Complaining, actually. Yammering on until he thought his bloody head would explode. Fortunately, he'd found a solution to mute her or he'd be in serious danger of going mad.

They only had a few hours until nightfall. The nearest inn was still half a day's journey away. Which meant they'd be sleeping in the heather for the night. That was sure to please his shrew of a wife. He had no doubt within ten seconds of them stopping, she'd be cursing him to the devil.

He pulled his horse off the path and guided it through the trees until he found a likely looking campsite. A creek ran nearby, and a small crop of rocks would provide some protection to their backs.

Before he even dismounted, Sorcha started in. He ignored her as best he could, though his solution wasn't foolproof. He could still hear her muffled shouts of his name. He sighed.

"It will be dark soon. We'll have to make camp here for the night."

"What do you mean, here? The devil take you, Malcolm MacGregor! I'll not spend the night sleeping in the dirt like some common hoyden."

Heh. It only took five seconds.

He dismounted and tied up his horse while she went off on a long tirade that he did his best to ignore. But since he wasn't a total heathen and his mother would box his ears for failing to help a lady, he did raise his arms to offer assistance in dismounting her horse.

She looked as though she'd slap his hand away, but then she peered closer at him. Her jaw dropped in outrage and she drew in a deep breath to let fly a stream of insults he was glad he could only half hear.

"Remove them! Remove them at once!" she shouted at him.

Removing the balls of linen he'd packed in his ears to drown her out was the last thing he wanted to do but her shrill shouting would alert every animal and brigand within a fifty mile radius of their location. And while the animals might be frightened away by the din she created, the brigands wouldn't be. Though he had half a mind to find them himself and turn her over. Or find a nice parcel of Campbell raiders and pay them to take her back to her father. Mayhap the king would take pity on him and lock him in a nice, dark cell somewhere out of her reach.

He reluctantly pulled the linen from his ears, resisting the urge to flinch when she started in again.

"Madam, if you dinna stop that fearful caterwauling ye'll have every bandit in the country raining down upon us."

That surprisingly shut her up. For the moment.

"I thought the roads were safe. We haven't seen another soul in the last three days."

"For the most part, they are. But there's always the danger of running afoul of someone who means to do ye harm. I'd as soon not let anyone who might be so inclined know of our position. Which means ye need to keep quiet."

She pursed her lips together, her cheeks flushing with fury. And just as suddenly, her face crumpled and her eyes filled with tears.

"I'm sorry. It's only that I'm so tired and cold and it's been such a long journey already and I don't have any of my things or my maid and now we have to sleep on the ground."

She sniffed loudly and unhooked her leg from the pommel. Only instead of hopping to the ground, she slid off in a boneless heap and landed square on her bum in the dirt. Which set off the tears again.

Malcolm rubbed his hand over his eyes. "Jesus, Mary, and Joseph, save me from this woman," he muttered. An all out war with her clan was preferable to spending his life married to such a creature. Unfortunately, despite how miserable she obviously was, she'd yet to tell him to take her home.

He walked over to her, then stepped over her to take her horse's bridle.

"That's a good laddie," he murmured to the horse, completely ignoring the furious sputtering of his sweet wife. "Did the nasty blethering woman scare ye, now?"

He led the horse to the branch near his own mount and tied him up. Before he could turn around, a clod of dirt struck him in the back. He squared his shoulders and slowly turned around, on guard for further projectiles.

"Are you going to leave me here in the muck?" she screeched.

"Aye, the thought had crossed my mind. Ye look so comfortable there. I thought ye'd like a wee rest after riding for so long. I've heard of nothing else since this morn."

"You didn't hear anything! You had your ears stopped up. I knew you were no gentleman, but I didn't think even you would stoop so low as to treat me in such a manner!"

"And what manner would that be?" he asked, kicking a space clear where he could build a fire. "Not announcing to the king and the entire court that ye'd attempted to murder me on our wedding night? Keeping ye as wife after such behavior and saving ye and yer entire family from the disgrace that would come from rejecting ye the morning after we'd wed? That would ha' set some tongues wagging, I assure ye. Or perhaps ye mean during this journey when I've kept ye clothed, fed, and safeguarded, though yer wicked tongue tempts me to leave ye by the roadside for whoever would dare take ye."

Sorcha got to her feet and flicked her skirts, shaking as much dust out of them as she could. Then she stalked over to him and stood toe to toe. She only reached his shoulder but she planted her hands on her hips and cursed at him like she was a warrior standing several feet taller. He waited until she ran out of steam before attempting to speak.

"Are ye finished?" he asked with a weary sigh.

"Oh!" she said, stomping her foot for good measure. "Stop acting as though you are so persecuted. *I* am the one in an intolerable situation, and I'm simply trying to make do with my circumstances as best as I can."

"Nay, madam. That I doubt. I have seen ye with others. You are kind and soft spoken and polite and altogether pleasant, in general. It seems to be me who brings out the shrew in you."

"Well, and whose fault is that?"

"And in case ye missed it," he said, ignoring that question completely, "ye're not the only one in an intolerable situation."

"No, but you weren't forced into a new life!" she said, her eyes growing shiny with tears again. Only this time, Malcolm didn't think they were pretense.

"You didn't have to leave your home, or your family, or your friends, or your belongings and travel with a man who now has complete charge over your very life, a man who has made it clear, in no uncertain terms, how little regard he has for you." She took a deep breath and straightened her backbone. "I know you didn't want this marriage any more than I. But at the end of this journey, you'll be home. And I'll be in a pit of vipers who would welcome any misfortune that may befall me. So you'll have to forgive me, if my temper is somewhat foul."

Shame crept through him at her words. Aye, she might have been trying to make his life a misery apurpose. But he couldn't really say he blamed her. He still couldn't imagine a lifetime of being tied to a woman who seemed hell-bent on his misery. But he could relent a bit, at least for the moment.

"My apologies, Sorcha," he said, placing his hand over his heart and giving her a small bow. "Ye do indeed bear the heavier burden. And for tonight, at least, I'll no' make it worse."

She blinked at him, eyes wide with surprise. She opened her mouth to respond and then snapped it shut again, her brow slightly furrowed. She didn't seem to know what to say to that.

He quickly made a fire and then stood and brushed off his hands. "I'll find us some supper. Here." He pulled a dagger out of his boot and handed it to her hilt first. "I willna go far, but stay near the fire and keep this with ye. Shout if ye need me. But...do remember I'm trying to catch our evening meal so if ye shout for no reason, we might be going to bed with empty bellies tonight."

She snorted and tucked the dagger into her belt. "I'll keep that in mind."

"I'll be right back," he said, his lips pulling into a small smile.

Chapter Ten

Sorcha watched him disappear into the foliage. As soon as he was gone, she sank onto a log with a great sigh. Playing the shrew was exhausting work. She'd had a governess once who had never been satisfied with anything. Nothing Sorcha had done would please her. Sorcha had soon realized the woman just enjoyed being miserable and even more, enjoyed making everyone around her equally as miserable. What Sorcha hadn't realized was the amount of energy it took to be so unpleasant all the time. She was glad Malcolm had called a bit of a truce for the evening. She needed a break.

He was never going to give up. She'd thought for sure he'd turn back after the first day. For certain after the first week. Yet the week had passed and still he'd sat upon his horse, day in and day out, listening to her petty complaints and dealing with her tantrums and somehow managing to not kill her. She was impressed, despite herself. Because at this point, she didn't have half his patience with herself.

Oh, he gave nearly as good as he got. She was fairly certain he was employing the same tactic as she—drive the other away and get out of the marriage while the other party took the blame. But, if neither one of them gave in, then what? They would continue to badger each other until one of them died? That sounded like a wretched way to spend her life.

But what choice did she have? Each day took her further from everything she held dear, further into enemy territory where who-knew-what awaited her.

A rustling sounded in the leaves, and she sighed. Time to play the shrew again.

She stood up and brushed off her skirts, planting the sourest expression she could muster on her face. "It's about time you…"

Her voice trailed away as she looked up and saw that the man who appeared was not Malcolm. Nor any of his men. This man had obviously been living rough for some time. His unkempt beard was full of brambles and twigs, his clothes in tatters. He came slowly toward her. The way his gaze crept over her body made her skin crawl and a shiver run up her spine. He hadn't said a word, yet she knew he was there to do her harm.

"Stay there," she said, pulling the dagger from her belt. She silently blessed Malcolm, an act she never thought she'd commit, for leaving it for her.

The sight of the blade stopped the man momentarily, but all too soon he began to stalk her again. He slowly circled the campsite, inching a little nearer with each circuit. She copied his movements, keeping the fire between them. That, unfortunately, didn't deter him. He leapt over the fire and was on her before she could run.

She screamed and thrashed beneath him, trying to get her arm from under him so she could use the dagger she clutched.

"Malcolm!" she screamed again, before the man slammed a hand over her mouth.

"Don't want ye bringing yer man back here just yet, now

do we?" He grabbed a filty rag out of his pocket and jammed it in her mouth so far she gagged, though she tried desperately not to vomit. The bastard on top of her didn't seem like he cared whether or not she choked to death.

"Now, we're going to get up nice and quiet," he said, leaning over so his acrid breath washed over her face. "And then we'll go find a nice out-of-the-way spot where I can take my time going through those bags."

Sorcha redoubled her grip on the dagger. She wasn't going anywhere with him. He might be interested in the horses and whatever they carried that might be of value, but she had no doubt his interest would eventually turn to her. And she had no intention of letting that happen. Since Malcolm had apparently not kept his word and wandered too far off to help her, she'd have to save herself.

The man heaved off her and hauled her up by the neck. She didn't fight him. Instead, she got a good grip on her dagger and used the momentum of his pull to help drive the blade home. The dagger sank into his belly, though she didn't know how much damage it would inflict considering the size of his gut. It did, however, wound him enough that he howled and released his hold on her. She yanked the cloth from her mouth, spitting to try to rid herself of the foul taste, and scrambled away, her throat throbbing.

"Malcolm!" she screamed again, as loud as she could, though the sound came out strangled and raw.

The man shouted and made to lunge after her, but before he could, Malcolm sprang from the bushes, a dagger in one hand, a sword in the other, roaring with fury.

The man's face lost all color. "*Leòmhann*," he muttered.

Oh yes. Malcolm, with his hair flying about his head, his teeth bared as he bore down on his prey, looked almost more beast than man. Lion, indeed. But he was *her* lion.

The brigand hefted his own blade but moved toward

Sorcha again, obviously intent on using her as a shield. Before he could take two steps, Malcolm's dagger whistled through the air and lodged itself to the hilt in the man's neck. He dropped to his knees. And then to his side. He didn't move again.

Sorcha slumped to the ground, her chest heaving as she tried to drag in a breath. Malcolm rushed to her.

He gathered her to him, his hands running over her, lingering at her throat.

"Are ye hurt?"

She slapped his hands away and tried to stand up. "No. I'm fine. And you're late."

His eyes widened. "I'm late, am I?"

He helped her get to her feet and her legs still shook enough that she let him, though she pushed away from him as soon as she was able. The only thing she wanted to do was curl up in his arms and let him hold her for a few minutes. But that would be giving into her weakness and revealing it to Malcolm. Two things she most definitely did not want to do. So she took a few steadying breaths and brushed off her skirts.

"Yes. Late. I screamed for you ages ago."

An amused half-smile broke out on his lips. "My apologies, my lady. I did arrive a bit earlier than I let on, but didna want to risk your safety and so waited 'til I was certain I could wound him without also wounding you."

She briefly glanced at him but quickly looked away. He stared at her with too much concern. Like he could see past the pretense that she was fine. She'd never needed a hug so badly in her entire life, but she'd be damned if she asked for one.

"Well," she said, trying to clear the raspy rattle from her throat, "I suppose that makes sense. I do appreciate not being struck through with a blade."

Malcolm's grin grew wider, though he still watched her with careful, wary eyes. "Ye're welcome."

"Just...try not to wander so far afield again. I might not be able to do half your job for you next time." She gestured to the knife sticking from the man's side, her voice cracking.

"Aye, lass," he said, reaching for her as if to brush her hair from her face, but letting his hand drop before touching her. "I'll keep that in mind."

"Good." Her hands twisted in her skirts, but the furious pounding of her heart had calmed somewhat and she was able to draw larger breaths of air.

Malcolm watched her a moment more and then turned and went back toward the trees from where he'd appeared. "Here," he said, coming back and handing her a water skin. "I thought ye might be thirsty. I gathered some fresh water."

"Thank you." She grabbed the skin and brought it hastily to her lips, gulping down the clear, cool water.

Malcolm hovered over her for a minute until her glares finally seemed to take effect and he left her be to deal with the dead man in their camp. He hastily went through the man's pockets but didn't find anything of note. There was no horse nearby, nor any sign that anyone else was in the area. Still, Sorcha didn't feel safe staying where they were.

Malcolm made quick work of the rabbit he'd caught, and they ate in silence, though Sorcha couldn't stomach more than a few bites. He pulled an oatcake with cranberries and caraway seeds from his sporran and offered it to her.

She took it, hoping it would settle her belly, but one bite of it and she handed it back.

"Ye didna care for it?" he asked, in genuine surprise.

"It's good. I'm just...not up to food at the moment."

"Are ye sure?"

At her nod he shrugged and popped the whole cake in his mouth. She couldn't help but smile at the pleased grin on his face as he chewed.

"Enjoy those, do you?"

"Oh, aye. They're no' so bad with a bit of blackberry, or even plain. But nothing like a nice, tart cranberry and a few caraway seeds."

"I'll have to keep that in mind. When I'm feeling better."

Malcolm offered her another leg of the rabbit but she waved it away. He wrapped it in a bit of leather and stared quietly into the fire for a few moments.

"Do ye think ye can ride for a bit longer?"

She raised an eyebrow. "Tonight?"

"Aye. He willna trouble us anymore," he said, nodding toward the woods where he'd disposed of the body, "but I'd feel better putting some distance between us. There's an inn a few hours ride from here, if ye think ye can manage."

Sorcha nodded, though she was weary down to her very bones. "I can ride. Is it safe, though?"

"Aye, safe enough. We'll stay off the road, stick to the trees. The moon is bright enough we willna be stumbling about in the dark."

"All right then."

They packed quickly and mounted, leaving the glen behind them. Sorcha wasn't sure how long she lasted before her eyes grew heavy and her head began to slump. She jerked awake with a gasp twice before Malcolm drew his horse up beside hers and plucked her from her saddle, setting her before him on his horse.

"What are you doing?" she demanded.

"Making sure you dinna fall off your horse or fall asleep and let him wander off with ye unaware on his back." He took her reins and tied them to his pommel to lead her horse.

She struggled to sit up away from him, though in truth the warm circle of his arms was about the most heavenly thing she'd felt in a long time.

"Rest yer head, lass. Ye've had a long day. I'll no' let ye fall," he said quietly, wrapping his plaid about them both.

Sleep pulled at her, and she finally relented with a sigh.

"All right, but only because I don't want you leaving me for dead along the side of the road. That would be entirely too convenient for you, and I have no intention of making your life convenient."

His chuckle rumbled deep in his chest and reverberated through her own.

"Nay worries, my wife. Convenient ye are not."

Her lips twitched at that. She rested her head against his chest once again, confused at the conflicted feelings pummeling her. Her main goal had been to be the biggest inconvenience possible. His words should have made her happy. Her plan was working. The poor man looked harried, worried, and ready to pull out his hair. By the time they reached his home, he should be sending a messenger post haste to the king, offering his surrender.

So why did her stomach feel as though it was sinking to the bottom of her shoes?

Chapter Eleven

Every bone in Sorcha's body ached. They'd been traveling for two weeks, and while she'd been anxious about reaching her new home, at this point, she'd have gladly curled up with a family of wolves, if it meant she could get off her horse.

Malcolm had ridden ahead a few yards and waited for her at the top of the hill they'd been traveling. There was a new energy about him, an excitement that hadn't been there earlier. She spurred her horse to a trot so she could catch up. The top of the hill was an excellent vantage point for the valley below. A loch appeared in the distance before them, its waters glistening in the late afternoon sun. A small village spread out to the left, its lanes bustling with people going about their tasks.

And to the right stood Glenlyon Castle. Or what was left of it. The back section looked as though a cannon ball had blasted through the surrounding wall, decimating one tower and part of the building. The rest of the structure appeared sound. It didn't have the ramparts and pepper-pot towers of some of the palaces she'd stayed in during her travels. But it was a commanding presence nonetheless, with its large square main building rising to tower above the rest of the structure.

"Welcome to Glenlyon," Malcolm said. "Try not to burn it down."

He spurred his horse forward, and Sorcha bit her tongue to keep from cursing at his retreating back. Stubborn bastard. She'd never thought to make it to Glenlyon's gates. The man either had more patience than God himself or was the most stubborn creature to ever walk beneath the sun. Either way, she was now stuck in the wilderness with a man who wanted nothing to do with her. No help for it but to keep up her antics and hope if she couldn't drive him to break their marriage, she could at least drive him away from her. Her mother had lived happily separated from her father, aside from the once or twice a year he had deigned to visit. Sorcha saw no reason why she and Malcolm couldn't live in a similar way. Hopefully, with her firmly ensconced back in London. Or, at the very least, Edinburgh.

She urged her horse into a trot to catch up with Malcolm and tried to calm the desperate fluttering of her stomach. She was about to enter a MacGregor stronghold. So far, it looked nothing like the bowels of hell her family would have her believe. In fact, she could easily be entering any of her father's or uncles' estates.

As they passed through the village lanes below the castle walls, people ran up to greet Malcolm. Some handed him goods, a loaf of bread fresh from the ovens or a hastily picked heather blossom. Malcolm smiled and chatted with everyone who approached him, though it was obvious he was anxious to be home.

They rode through the gates of the castle to more cheers and waves. Malcolm glanced at her and scowled at the puzzled expression she probably hadn't hidden.

"What?" he asked.

Sorcha shrugged. "Merely surprised, that's all. These people all seem to like you."

Malcolm laughed. "Aye? And that's cause for surprise, eh?"

"They must not know you as well as I do." She smiled sweetly, and he laughed again.

"Ye dinna ken me as well as ye think ye do, wife. I'm quite pleasant to be around when my life or my virtue isna in constant danger."

Sorcha's jaw dropped. "Your virtue?"

"Aye! I see the way ye look at me at night when ye think I sleep."

Sorcha sputtered. "Well I never...I don't know what you're talking about."

Malcolm chuckled again, a deep sound of male pride that she wished she could strangle from his throat. He wasn't wrong, damn him. But he didn't need to gloat so.

"I can assure you, your virtue is quite safe from me. And as for your life, you really need to let that go. It was an accident. If I'd wanted you dead, you'd be dead."

His eyes searched hers for a moment before turning back to the path ahead of them that wound up through the inner castle walls to the keep. "Aye, I suppose that's true enough. Ye might accidentally trip and drown me in the privy. Or perhaps inadvertently swipe a knife through my gullet while trying to clean the blade. Or push me off a cliff during a sudden, uncontrollable sneezing fit."

"You really are too fond of your own voice," she said, resisting the urge to take off her shoe to throw at him. She ignored his answering laugh.

They entered the main courtyard and pulled to a stop. The area bustled with all manner of people busy with their chores, all who greeted their laird. And arranged at the bottom of the steps leading inside the massive wooden doors were what must be the household staff, though there were barely ten people all together. How was a place as large as Glenlyon Castle managed by so few?

A tall, thin woman stood at the head of the line, a broad smile on her wrinkled face.

"Welcome home, my lord," she said, with a small curtsy.

"Ah, Mrs. Byrd!" He grabbed her in a huge bear hug and swung her around. "It's good to be back."

Sorcha watched this display with undisguised astonishment. The man actually sounded…happy. Jovial, even. Speaking in a tone she'd never heard from him. Which brought home how miserable he must have been with her. That was the plan, of course, but for some reason, the thought still hurt.

She adjusted her skirts to slide off her horse when a handsome, smiling man only slightly smaller than Malcolm appeared at her side. He held up his hands to help her down, and she reached for him gratefully. Normally, she'd have dismounted as gracefully as she could on her own, if only to prove to Malcolm she could. However, his entire household was currently staring at her, as if she'd sprouted two heads. So falling on her face in the dirt wasn't something she wished to do just then.

She braced herself on the man's shoulders and let him lift her down.

"Thank you," she said. "I don't know your name but you were at court with Lord Glenlyon, were you not?" She'd seen him with Malcolm's men at the start of their journey as well, but he hadn't been one of the ones dancing attendance on her.

"Aye, mistress. I'm the laird's cousin. The name is John MacGregor, at your service." John swept off his bonnet and gave her an elegant bow. She couldn't help but smile.

"All right, be gone with ye," Malcolm said, shooing his cousin away with a good-natured scowl.

John gave her a wink. "Welcome to yer new home, my lady."

Her stomach dropped at those words but she nodded graciously. As soon as John was out of earshot, Malcolm turned back to her and leaned down to whisper to her.

"Ye've made it abundantly clear how ye feel about me, madam, and if ye insist on taking out your misery on me, so be it. But I'll no' let ye abuse my people. So I'll warn ye now…"

Sorcha pulled away from him, anger burning away the last of her unease. "I know you think I'm nothing but a spoiled shrew, but I'd never punish your people for your sins. As long as they do naught to me, they'll have naught to fear from me. Fair?"

Malcolm nodded. "You are my wife. They'll treat ye with the respect that title deserves."

The respect the title deserved. Not that she deserved. She sighed. No more than to be expected, especially as it was her own doing. Still, for the thousandth time, she wished things could be different.

Malcolm introduced her to the staff, most of whom eyed her warily. She couldn't blame them, she supposed. But she heartily wished Berta was at her side. It would have been good to have one friendly face.

Mrs. Byrd curtseyed and then turned to Malcolm. "I'm sorry, my lord, but I'm afraid yer lady's chamber isna ready quite yet."

Malcolm frowned. "Didna John bring word it was to be opened?"

"Oh aye, of course. But there was a fair bit of damage to the roof from the last storm, and some of the furniture was rotting from the damp. I've had that removed, and new items are being located. The room is being aired and, of course, the roof replaced, as we speak, but I'm afraid it'll be another day or so afore it's ready."

Malcolm sighed. "Nay matter. I'll be leaving in the morning, in any case. She can stay in my chamber until her suite is ready."

"You're leaving?" Sorcha asked. Perhaps her bad behavior was finally beginning to pay off.

"No need to sound so pleased about it," Malcolm said, though she thought she detected some amusement hastily buried. "I've been gone near two months. I need to see to my estate. Why?" he asked, suddenly pulling her in against him and leaning down as if to kiss her. "Will ye miss me when I'm gone, lass?"

"Let me go, you big oaf," she said, squirming against him.

There was some amused laughter from their audience that quickly disappeared. She dodged Malcolm's lips again and glanced around for help, but they'd been left alone.

"Sorry, love, no one around but the two of us."

"Let me go," she said, hauling her foot back to kick his shin.

He grunted and released her, though she doubted he'd even felt anything.

"What am I supposed to do while you're off roaming whatever pile of sticks you call an estate? Sit here and stare at the rain dripping through the ceiling?"

"Aye, if it suits ye," he said, wandering over to a sideboard against the wall that held a pitcher of ale and several glasses. He poured himself a healthy glass and drank it down. "I dinna care much what you do as long as ye dinna disrupt my household."

She grabbed a cup and threw it at him. He calmly ducked and poured himself another drink.

"If ye keep throwing all our glasses, we'll have naught to drink from and will have to resort to drinking straight from the bottle at every meal."

Another cup followed the first, and Malcolm sighed. "Lord save me from aggravating women."

He finished his ale and flung his plaid back around his shoulders.

"Aggravating women? Surely you jest! I have never met a more disagreeable, ill-mannered, unwashed, unkempt, beast of a man in all my days!"

He sniffed in the general direction of his armpit and recoiled. "Aye, I am a bit ripe at that. Nay matter. I can bathe in the loch while I'm making my rounds. Still plenty of daylight left."

He turned to head back out the door.

"You're leaving now?" she said, hurrying after him. "I thought you were leaving in the morning."

"Madam, I'd rather sleep naked in the rain atop a hill of goat dung than spend one more moment in yer delightful company." He tipped his hat to her and turned to march off.

"That…that… Ooh!" she said, blowing out a furious breath.

A servant boy bustled by with a bundle of sticks under his skinny arms, probably headed for the kitchen. Sorcha grabbed one from his pile, ignoring his gasp of surprise and threw it at Malcolm's retreating back. It glanced off his shoulder, but did make him pause long enough to glance back at her.

"Practice your aim while I'm gone, lass. 'Tis hardly fitting for the laird's wife to miss so often."

Sorcha's jaw dropped, but unfortunately there was nothing left to throw at him. Not that she could hit him on his thick, Scottish head anyway. She did need to work on her aim. Damn him. She stomped back inside the keep.

Her fury faded as she stood inside the cavernous hall and realized she had no idea where her chamber — or his chamber, rather — was located. Though now that she was alone she could look at her new home a bit more thoroughly. She'd been too preoccupied when she'd first entered to notice much.

It was a small keep, as castles went. The entire thing could probably fit inside her father's smallest holding. Still, it was sturdily built, and grand for its size. The main hall was obviously used for a multitude of purposes. There was a table set up on a dais at the head of the hall, where the family must take their meals. Other tables and benches were pushed along the side walls, clearing the main floor. She supposed they were brought out during meal times. The hall could probably accommodate two hundred people, though she somehow doubted that many regularly dined there, if any did at all.

The entire place needed a good airing and cleaning. The rushes on the floors should have been changed ages ago. Threadbare and damaged tapestries needed to be cleaned or repaired. The chandeliers were covered in wax and there were birds living in the rafters that should be chased out before any more of their droppings could decorate the hall. If this is what the main hall of the manse looked like, she shuddered to think what the rest of the building might hold.

"My lady?"

Sorcha turned at the timid inquiry. "Has Lord Glenlyon left?"

A mousy but sturdy looking maid came the rest of the way into the room. "Aye, my lady. Just a few minutes ago."

"Excellent!"

The maid blinked, startled. "My lady?"

Sorcha took her first deep breath in weeks. "What is your name?"

Her eyes darted around, never rising to meet Sorcha's. The poor girl was as wary as a rabbit caught in a trap. "Mary, mistress."

"Mary, please gather the staff. We have work to do."

"Aye, mum," Mary said, scurrying off as fast as she could to do Sorcha's bidding.

Sorcha sighed. She'd have to treat Malcolm's people gently if she was to assure them she wasn't the enemy they likely feared. She only hoped they'd return the favor.

She glanced around the hall again. Like it or not, this was her home for now. She might as well make it livable.

Within an hour, she had the staff mobilized removing old rushes, taking down tapestries, and chasing cobwebs from the corner, and she sent to the village for more able bodies who were willing to work at the castle. While Malcolm's people were hesitant around her, they obeyed her orders readily enough, and most of their demeanors lightened once she'd shown she was willing to work beside them. She could easily imagine what they'd been expecting, and she was determined to prove them wrong.

Sorcha pulled a kerchief out of her pocket and tied up her hair, thankful, once again, for Malcolm's foresight in providing sturdier clothing. Not that she'd ever tell him that. Every dark corner she poked her nose into was covered in cobwebs and the last thing she wanted was a family of pests living in her carefully tended tresses.

The prospect of restoring the old hall to its former glory filled her with renewed energy. Malcolm might be right about some things. She'd been spoiled and pampered most her life, yes. But she also knew how to work when it was called for and had been trained since birth in the workings of running a large household. It was obvious from the state of his home that no one had been in charge in quite some time. That was about to change.

While the staff continued working on the hall, she had Mary take her to the bedchambers. Might as well see what nasty surprises they held.

Mary led her to a common sitting room that Sorcha was pleased to see was in much better condition than the hall below. A large fireplace stood opposite the door with comfortable chairs set before it. An ivory chess set was arranged on a small table near one of the lead-paned windows and a desk, Malcolm's, she assumed, sat near the opposite window. A door on each side of the room led to what she assumed were the sleeping chambers.

"Which is mine?" she asked.

Mary gestured to the left. "This way, my lady. But it's no' ready yet. There was some damage…"

"Yes, yes, I know. Mrs. Byrd explained all that. I simply want to inspect it."

"Aye, my lady."

Mary opened the door and stood back to let Sorcha enter. Sorcha shivered as a cold blast of air hit her and remembered that Mrs. Byrd had told her they were airing the rooms out. The chamber appeared about as Sorcha had expected. Furnished with sturdy but feminine-looking furniture, the linens in gentle shades of blue with several light-colored furs piled on the bed. The room was musty and covered in dust, but it would do nicely.

"Get a few girls in here to get it cleaned up. I'll sleep in the laird's chamber tonight but I'd like to be in my own room as soon as possible."

"Aye, mum," Mary said, with a little bob.

Sorcha turned and marched across the sitting room to Malcolm's chamber before her nerve could desert her, chastising herself for her silliness. It wasn't as though he was lying in wait for her. Quite the opposite. She'd literally chased him from his own hall. She couldn't stop a smile from breaking out at that thought. After a fortnight on the road, the mighty Laird of Glenlyon was going to spend his first night at home somewhere else—under the stars—rather than spend it with her. Which meant her plan was working.

In the meantime, she'd spend the night curled up in his massive bed surrounded by deep red velvet drapes and try not to think of how he'd look stretched out beside her. Those thoughts had no place in her marriage. And neither did she.

Chapter Twelve

Malcolm sat atop his horse gazing down at the castle below him.

"Anything wrong?" John asked, riding up beside him.

Malcolm's brow furrowed slight. "Nay. Not that I can tell. It's still standing, so that's a relief at least."

John laughed. "Och, come now. Ye didna actually expect the lass to destroy the place, did ye?"

Malcolm snorted. "Dinna underestimate her. I have no doubt she could pull the entire place apart stone by stone, if she put her mind to it."

"Ye say that almost as if ye admire her."

"I admire her the way one might admire a wild boar that has been cornered in the hunt. I can admire strength and grace and beauty without wanting to get anywhere near it."

John laughed deeply at that. "I'm sure my lady Glenlyon would love to hear herself compared to a cornered wild boar."

"Ye dinna know my lady," Malcolm said wryly.

He took a deep breath, savoring the crisp autumn air as it stole through his lungs. He'd sorely missed his home in the weeks he'd been away. Thankfully, there hadn't been anymore raids while they'd been gone, cementing his belief that Campbell had been behind them. But for the moment at least, it looked as though the truce bought with his marriage was affording them some sorely-needed peace. Perhaps it would be better to remain married to Sorcha, if peace really could be maintained. He could put up with her, if it meant his people could live their lives without fear. Of course, his personal life would be a never-ending battle. But the price would be worth it, for the sake of those who depended on him.

"Home then?" John asked.

"Aye. After we stop in at the tenants below the keep."

Malcolm had saved those nearest the castle for last as they were better protected against the raids and had easier access to the castle's resources should the need arise. So he didn't expect to find too many problems, though he still liked to make sure all was well.

Nothing, however, prepared him for what he found at the first cottage. Old Granny MacGregor had been old even when Malcolm was a child, and despite her resemblance to the twisted brambles that grew around her cottage, she was generally a jolly sort. Her mood that morning, however, was jovial, even for her. She welcomed him into her home with a face-splitting grin and hobbled over to the cheerily crackling fire to put on the kettle.

"Nay, Granny, dinna trouble yerself. We canna stay. I'm merely stopping in to be sure ye want for naught."

"Ah, such a good laddie," she said, patting his arm before settling herself into her chair by the fire. "Yer kind to think of old Granny, but her ladyship has already been by twice this week and set all to rights."

Malcolm's eyes widened. "Her ladyship?"

"Aye, that angel ye've marrit. Chosen well ye did, for all that she's a Campbell."

Malcolm stood frozen for a moment, too many thoughts running through his head to make sense of any of them. He opened his mouth but closed it again, struck speechless for the first time in his life. Surely she didn't refer to Sorcha?

John glanced at him, eyebrows raised, before turning back to Granny himself. "Set to rights? Was there ought amiss then?"

"Och, nothin' much. A small leak in the roof just there," she said motioning to a spot in the corner. "And things were a bit out of sorts with Maisri still in childbed."

"Oh, aye?" Malcolm said, shaking himself out of the stupor the news of Sorcha's actions had put him. "Her fourth now, is it?"

"Aye, and a bonny laddie he is, too. Takes after his grandfather, ye ken," she said, smiling fondly at the memory of her long departed husband. "All is well with mother and babe, but she's no' been able to come help the past few weeks. But her ladyship, she sent a girl from the keep to help with the cleaning up, even cooked me a bit o' supper. And the laddies fixed my roof right proper not a day ago. My lady has come to check on me every day. Why, ye only missed her by a few moments, truth be told. She left me with that basket of simples. Such a fine lady, she is. Fit for our laird, right enough."

Malcolm stared around the cottage at the gleaming surfaces, the pot of stew bubbling happily over the fire, and the enormous basket of supplies that did indeed sit overflowing on the table. Sorcha did all this? *His* Sorcha?

John stepped in again, rightly suspecting Malcolm was momentarily struck dumb with shock. He murmured a few kind words, with a promise to visit again soon, and led Malcolm out the door.

Once they were outside and mounted again, John removed a flask and handed it to Malcolm, who nodded his thanks and took a stiff drink.

"Do ye think she's gone daft?" Malcolm asked, handing it back.

John laughed and took his own swig. "That's the only explanation, is it?"

"Compared to Sorcha making rounds and seeing to my tenants? Aye, 'tis."

John laughed again and led his horse toward the next cottage.

They found the same at each home they visited. Maisri and her brood, including the new babe, had all been fed, cleaned, and left with baskets of goodies. Each and every cottage was warm, clean, and overflowing with content tenants and glowing reports of his angel of a wife.

Malcolm sat atop his horse, gazing into the distance at the last cottage they were to visit.

"Is it part of some plan, do ye think?" he asked.

John's eyebrow rose. "Plan to what? Kill them all with kindness?"

Malcolm snorted. "Aye. Or gain their favor so they'll back her when she finally succeeds in running me out o' my own home."

John chuckled and shook his head. "Or perhaps she's a kind-hearted lass deep down and ye just bring out the worst in her."

Malcolm sighed deeply. "Aye. That I'd believe. The bringing-out-the-worst-in-her part. Kind-hearted is a wee bit of a stretch."

He glanced up in time to catch sight of a woman exiting the distant cottage, followed by a girl, two sturdy lads, and one of the men from the castle. The man helped her into a waiting wagon and climbed in beside her. The others climbed in the back, and the wagon lurched off toward the castle.

"Is that her?" John asked.

Malcolm couldn't see her face at that distance, but he

caught a glimpse of raven ringlets beneath the hat she wore. "Seems so." Though he still couldn't believe the things his tenants had said about her. Such kindness, patience, and selflessness weren't part of the woman he knew and avoided. Not any part she'd ever shared with *him*, at least.

He spurred his horse forward. One more stop to make. One more tenant thrilled with a visit from both his lord and lady. One more tale of Christian goodness, angelic grace, and beauty.

Malcolm exited the cottage and turned his face to the afternoon sun. He took a deep breath, letting the brisk Highland breeze permeate his every cell.

"Well?" John asked.

Malcolm released a long breath. "Well. Either she's gone mad or I have. Either way, I could use some whisky, a warm fire, and a soft bed."

"Ye'll likely have to face your wife first."

"Aye. Well. Might as well get this over with. Let's go."

He spurred his horse forward, John following behind, his laugh ringing in the air.

The closer he got to the castle the more uneasy he became. The courtyard was bustling, with people scurrying about. Trestles had been set up where several men were pounding away at benches and stools.

Malcolm and John dismounted and handed their horses off to a boy who ran up to take them.

"What is happening here?" he said, glancing over at John who had a bemused expression on his face.

Malcolm took the stairs two at a time, coming to a dead halt when he reached the hall. It took a moment for his eyes to adjust to the dimmer surroundings and once they did, he wasn't sure he had come home to the right hall at all.

A veritable army of servants were organized into groups: some scrubbing at bird droppings on the walls and floors, others polishing every surface available until they gleamed. A trio of young girls giggled while they picked wax and polished the wood from the chandeliers that had been lowered. And over in the corner, closest to the roaring fireplace where the light was good, was his shrew of a wife, her hair in a kerchief, laughing and chatting with several of the village women as they worked on a tapestry.

"What is going on here?" he said, his voice booming over the industrious noise.

Everyone stopped in their tracks, hands poised midair as they turned to look at him in the sudden silence.

Almost as one, their eyes turned to Sorcha who had extracted herself from her group and was hurrying toward him.

"You're back," she said, once she reached him, planting her hands on her hips and looking down with dismay at his muddy boots. "And tracking mud all over my hall, as well."

"Yer hall?"

"Timothy!" Sorcha called out, ignoring him.

A small lad of about ten ran over with a rag and pail in his hands. "Aye, mum?"

"Please mop up this mess so the laird can move about without destroying all our hard work."

"Aye, mum," Timothy said with a huge grin.

Before Malcolm could say a word, the lad had knelt down and quickly wiped down his boots and the surrounding floor.

"Thank you, Timothy," Sorcha said, ruffling his hair. "Why don't you run along to the kitchens and see if Mrs. Byrd has any treats for you. You've been working so hard today."

"Aye, mum, thank 'ee."

"Sorcha, what in the devil—"

"Not here," she said. She turned and marched up the stairs, gathering her skirts in her hands, her pert little bottom swaying as she jogged up the steps.

He glanced at John who was accepting a mug of ale from a flirtatious maid. Malcolm nearly rolled his eyes and turned to follow his wife.

He entered his sitting room and stopped midstride. The entire room had been rearranged. The chess table now sat between the arm chairs at the fireplace, his desk had been moved closer to his own chamber near the largest window which, he could see now, afforded it the best light. And the whole place shone and gleamed and gave off a pleasant, polished scent.

"Will you please explain what is going on here?" he said, his heart thundering in his chest.

She handed him a glass of whisky. "Sit down so I can get those boots off before you destroy the rug."

He opened his mouth to protest and then glanced down at the cup in his hand, his eyebrow raised.

Sorcha sighed, exasperated. "It's not poisoned."

"Forgive me if I dinna take your word for it."

She cursed under her breath. "Give it to me." She grabbed it and took a quick sip before handing it back. "Satisfied?"

"About the whisky, maybe," he said, trying to keep from smiling at the blush that rushed to her cheeks. Whether from the whisky, her anger, or the run up the stairs, he wasn't sure. But by all the saints, the woman was breathtaking when she was riled.

She pushed him into a chair, and he held the cup aloft to keep it from spilling. She made quick work of removing his boots and propping them by the fire and then took her own seat across from his.

"Now," she said, straightening her skirts and folding her hands in her lap. "What seems to be the trouble?"

He put the whisky down on the table beside him, and then did a double take. "Where did this table come from?"

"The attic. I believe you were about to tell me why you

marched in blustering and shouting over nothing."

"Over nothing? I've been gone near a week and return to find my home unrecognizable!"

Sorcha nodded. "You're welcome. Now, if that's all, I have work to do."

"Nay, that's not all. What do you mean, you're welcome? That wasna a compliment!"

One delicate, dark eyebrow slowly rose. "Well, I choose to take it as one. You brought me here and then abandoned me within an hour. The castle was near falling down around our ears, hadn't been decently cleaned in more years than I care to consider, the furniture was falling apart, there were more birds in the hall than people, more droppings than mortar on the walls, and there wasn't a dry, clean surface to eat or sleep or prepare food in the entire castle! In a week, I've transformed this place from a dilapidated disaster into a warm, inviting home one can be proud of. And all you can do is shout at me?"

"Where did all the servants come from?"

"The village, of course."

"And how are we going to pay them for their labors? I dinna know what misconceptions ye may be under, but I'm no' a wealthy man, Sorcha. I dinna have the means to fund an entire renovation and keep half the village employed here."

"Oh, posh," she said, waving away his concerns. "It's hardly half the village and most of them are only here for a few days until we finish up the most pressing tasks. The men fixing the roof should be done tomorrow, or the next day at the latest—"

"There are men fixing the roof?"

"Of course," she said with an impatient sigh. "Stop interrupting. As I was saying, they should be finished shortly, the carpenters are working on the last of the benches now, and the rest is really more a matter of cleaning than repairing and I've only hired a few extra girls for that. Really I'm quite impressed at how much we've been able to accomplish in so short a time."

So was he, truth be told. But the last thing he wanted to do was inflate her ego. And the fact that she'd marched in and taken over without breaking stride didn't sit well with him.

"Are you truly angry that I've brought some order in and cleaned a few rooms?" she asked, staring at him with a mixture of anger, hurt, and disbelief that made him want to soothe her ruffled feathers.

He squashed the urge. "This is my home. Who gave ye permission to make changes and order everyone about as if…"

She nodded as he trailed off. "That's right. As if I were the lady of the castle. The wife of the laird. This is my home now, too, Malcolm, though I'm fully aware you loathe my presence. But you brought me here and then abandoned me without a backward glance. I had no idea if, or when, you'd return. So what was I supposed to do? Huddle in a corner beneath the filth and pretend I didn't exist? I'm not going to apologize for taking my rightful place here or for making the home where I'm to live more tolerable."

Malcolm sighed and rubbed his hand over his face. Exhaustion ate at him. They'd ridden hard to reach Glenlyon and while he'd taken time making the rounds around his lands, he'd longed for his own bed and the comfort of a few days of rest. Coming home to find things changed and Sorcha firmly ensconced in the role that had once been held by his mother, while his people sang her praises, had taken him by surprise. But she was right. Damn her.

"I apologize," he said, his voice low and deep with weariness.

She blinked up at him. "Excuse me?"

"I apologize," he said, with a small smile. "It's not

something I say often and I'll no' say it again now so take it or leave it."

She returned his wry smile. "I'll take it. And consider forgiving you. Maybe."

He snorted. "It wasna what I expected to find when I arrived home. And I meant it about my finances. Glenlyon has rich pasture lands, and we do well enough with our cattle, but with the raids of late, we've no' brought in so much as usual and a poor season of crops meant more who needed aid. The castle is in sore need of repair, I ken, but I'm afraid the work ye've commissioned…"

She waved him off again. "I told you, I've only ordered enough done to keep the place from completely falling about our ears. Necessary repairs and cleaning only. The women were happy to lend a hand with the tapestry, and we can easily accommodate a few new maids. The other repairs and workmen I paid for out of my own purse. It cost you nothing."

Malcolm almost flinched at that. "A man has his pride."

"Yes, I'm aware. Women often have the pleasure of bearing the brunt of a man's bruised ego. Like it or not, I'm your wife and I'm sure part of the reason you agreed to the marriage was the dowry I brought with me. Consider it part of what is owed you, if you wish. I, for one, consider it well spent, if I can rest in comfort without worrying about being doused with the first rain storm that passes overheard."

Malcolm released a long breath. "Aye, then. But from now on, I expect to be included in any decisions regarding the castle. Ye may be the lady here, wife, but I am the laird."

"If you insist," she said, inclining her head.

"I insist." He pushed himself up from the chair. "And now, I want nothing more than a wash and my bed."

"Oh, there is one more thing…"

Before she could finish, he'd pushed open the door to his chamber. Sorcha had obviously been hard at work here, too.

The rushes that usually adorned his floor had been replaced with a large rug and everything had been newly washed or polished. There were also signs of Sorcha everywhere. Hair combs and brushes on a table, sweet smelling flowers in a vase near the bed, a book lying open on the bedside table, and various bits and pieces of clothing that hadn't been put away yet.

He turned and glanced at her. "If ye wanted to be in my bed, all ye had to do was ask," he said.

Her cheeks flushed, and his belly tightened. He clenched his hands against the sudden urge to carry her over to his bed and have a proper homecoming.

"It's not what you think," she said, backing away from him a step as though she could read his thoughts. He followed her, backing her farther into the room.

"Nay?"

"As I said, I didn't know when, or if, you'd return and the roof over my chamber still needs to be repaired. I was comfortable enough here and wanted the worst to be repaired first. The workers are repairing the last of the damage over the hall today and should be able to repair my roof tomorrow."

"Hmm, and in the meantime, ye've been sleeping in my bed."

He'd backed her up against one of the four posters of the bed, and she bumped against it with a little squeak. Instead of pushing him away, though, she raised her impertinent little nose in the air.

"Yes. But now that you are home I shall make other arrangements. I'm certain a pallet on the floor somewhere will suffice."

"Och, no. We canna have the lady of the castle sleeping on a lowly pallet. There is more than enough room for us both in my bed."

She smiled up at him. Her sweet smile momentarily

caught him off guard. Her gaze dropped to his lips and lingered before slowly traveling back to meet his own, and the heat in those eyes hit him like a fist to the chest.

"Oh, I have no intention of sleeping on a pallet, my lord."

She rose up on tip toe and trailed one finger along his jaw line.

"Nay?"

Sorcha shook her head and bit her lip, and most of the blood in his body rushed south.

She looked up at him through a thick fringe of lashes, her sparkling blue eyes staring deep into his. A quick, gasping breath had her breasts straining against the laces of her dress.

She placed her hands on his chest…and pushed him as hard as she could, her foot lashing out to connect sharply with his leg. He stumbled backward, and she escaped, storming toward the door.

"The pallet is for you!" she called over her shoulder. "I'll send up some water. I have no desire to share a bedchamber with a man who reeks of horse and sweat."

Malcolm hopped back until he collided with the bed and sat down heavily. The door to the outer chamber slammed, and he started laughing. Finally, he lay back and flung his arm over his face.

"What am I going to do wi' that woman?" he said.

"Ye might start with bedding her good and well. I've never seen a woman more in need of a good tumble than that one."

Malcolm sat up and scowled at John. "Don't you ever knock?"

John shrugged. "If I knocked ye'd only tell me to go away and that wouldna do me any good."

Malcolm lay back on his bed. "Go away."

Instead, John sauntered into the room and collapsed into a chair, stretching his legs out. "Ye really are the most stubborn man alive, ye know that, don't ye?"

Malcolm snorted. "I dinna ken what ye mean."

"Aye, ye do, and that's my point exactly."

"I'm tired, John. Say what you will and have done with it so I can sleep."

"Ye're married to a beautiful, wealthy, spirited lass who in just a week has this place running as efficiently as any regiment and from the looks of things, has yer people eating out of the palm of her hand. And yet ye still complain."

Malcolm sighed. "I'll admit she's done a fair job with managing the household. But the woman wants nothing to do with me."

"So change her mind. Ye used to be a charming man, or so the lassies said. I'm sure some of that is still in ye somewhere."

Malcolm snorted again. "Go away, John." Then he peeked at him with one eye. "Were ye given your old chamber?"

John nodded. "Aye. Everything in it freshly cleaned, too. There's even a vase of flowers by my bed. I might never leave."

"Ye've been here since ye were eight years old, Cousin. I think ye can safely consider this your home."

John chuckled but before he could respond, the clanging of a bell rang out. Malcolm shot off the bed. The bell only rang if the castle or immediate vicinity was in danger.

Little Timothy burst into the chamber. "My lord! My lord!"

Malcolm was already in the sitting room pulling on his boots and buckling on his sword.

"What is it, lad?" he asked, running for the stairs, his exhaustion disappearing as his blood roared through him

Timothy ran quick on his heels. "A raid, my lord. Thomas Curly's flocks in the high pasture."

"John, gather the men," Malcolm said. John nodded and ran to the stables. Malcolm turned to see Sorcha standing with wide eyes in the hall. She hurried to him, following him out to the courtyard.

"If the raiders come to the castle or the village, our spotters will ring the warning bell. Get the women and children inside," he instructed her. "Bolt the doors and as soon as our men are gone, bar the gates. I'll leave some men here. Ye should be safe enough. I doubt they'd dare attack the castle—"

"But what about the south wall? With all the damage, won't it be easy for attackers—"

"Nay, dinna fash yerself, lass. The wall has been reinforced and is much stronger than it looks. The weak spot is near the east corner. The outer wall has only been superficially repaired there and won't hold under attack. I've keep extra men posted there, though, and none would know to look at. Ye'll be safe enough. And Thomas's fields aren't far off. To be cautious though…"

Sorcha nodded. "I'll make sure everyone is safe," she said, her face pale against the overcast sky.

Malcolm wanted to say much more. It was odd to have raiders come this close to the castle. He couldn't help but wondering if Sorcha's presence was making them bolder, or if it was perhaps a ruse to draw Malcolm away from the castle so Sorcha could then let them inside. Her fear seemed genuine though, and despite her hatred of him, he didn't think she'd willingly harm the innocent women and children who were in his care. Especially as she'd spent so much of her time looking after them.

John ran to them, leading their horses. Malcolm turned back to her. "Open the gates for none save myself or John."

She nodded again. "Be careful, my lord."

He could almost believe she meant that. With a great battle cry he turned and led his men out the gate, hoping they reached the high pasture in time.

Chapter Thirteen

Sorcha paced in her chamber. It had long since fallen dark, and still Malcolm and the others hadn't returned. She had watched from the battlements for a time. She couldn't see the skirmish, of course, but she could see the flames that leapt to the sky from the burning pastures. The wind carried the ashes toward them. But there was still no word from the men.

Despite herself, she was worried for the stubborn ox she'd married. She'd missed him when he'd left her immediately upon arriving at the castle. Missed their arguments. Missed the smiles he tried to hide when she was particularly riled. Missed his overbearing presence that somehow made her feel safe even while he was cursing her.

She'd grown accustomed to him, damn him. And she was so very weary of fighting the inevitable. They'd never love each other, but perhaps their lives didn't need to be filled with animosity. Glenlyon wasn't the viper pit she'd feared. She was starting to believe perhaps Malcolm wasn't the devil she'd feared either. She was at least willing to be civil enough to find out. If he ever returned home.

She finally sank, exhausted, into one of the chairs beside the fire and laid her head back to rest her eyes. A few moments later, the door opened, and she jumped up, her heart in her throat.

"Malcolm," she breathed, relief flooding her at the sight of his face, bloodied and dirty though it was. She hurried to him to take his sword.

"Mary!" she called out. Her maid poked her head from around the corner. "Bring hot water and linens."

Mary nodded, and Sorcha followed Malcolm to where he slumped into a chair. She propped up his sword by the table and bent to remove his boots.

"Ye dinna need to do that," he said, but she waved him off.

"Just be quiet and let me help," she ordered.

She bustled around him, making sure he was settled comfortably with a cup of ale, that she tasted before she handed to him just to save time to his apparent amusement. Mary brought water and a basin and handed a stack of small linens to Sorcha.

"Thank you, Mary. Is there a bathing tub?"

"Aye, mistress. Shall I have it brought up?"

"Yes, thank you."

Mary nodded and curtsied to them both before scuttling back out.

"A bath is too much bother," he insisted. "A quick wash will be fine."

"A quick wash will not be fine. You are filthy, covered in blood and heaven knows what else, and you smell as though you've been rolling in a pig sty. If I must sleep with you tonight, you will bathe."

He gave her an amused but exhausted smile. "I'm too tired to fight you tonight, lass. Do what ye will with me."

She snorted. "I don't think you have the strength, my

lord."

He peeked an eye open at that. "Och, aye? And what did ye—"

"Hush," she said, setting him off. His laughter was cut short with a hiss of pain, and fear spiked through Sorcha's heart.

"You're hurt?"

He waved her away. "It's naught but a scratch. I'll do."

"Let me see."

She yanked at his shirt, and he halfheartedly attempted to stop her.

"Stop with that, ye wee heathen. I like my clothes where they are."

"Well, that's too bad," she said, slapping his hand away and pulling up his shirt to expose his chest. The muscles in his stomach bunched and corded against the cool night air, his nipples pebbling into tiny rocks. Every line and plane of his body stood out in sharp, solid relief, and for a moment, she forgot why she was undressing him, lost in the beauty of his body.

"If ye've gotten enough of a peek, do ye mind if I remove the rest of the shirt? It's a bit hard to breathe this way."

She glanced up and realized she'd been holding the material up against his face as she admired his body. In her haste to cover her embarrassment she quickly yanked his shirt up and over his head, jarring his injured side in the process.

"Ah!" he gasped.

"Sorry," she murmured. Her stomach flipped uncontrollably though she wasn't sure if it was due to embarrassment or the fact that she was within touching distance of the most beautiful male chest she'd ever seen.

The main issue was immediately apparent. A gash the size of Sorcha's forearm was carved into his torso along the bottom of his ribcage.

"A scratch?" she asked, eyebrows raised. She went quickly to her small sewing basket and extracted a needle and the sturdiest thread she had and then grabbed the bottle of whisky on Malcolm's desk.

Malcolm took the opportunity to take a healthy swig or two of the whisky before Sorcha went to work cleaning and stitching the wound.

"Where did ye learn to do this?" Malcolm asked, nodding down at the neat stitches in his side.

Sorcha shrugged. "It's not so different from stitching material."

"Ye've done it before?"

"No. But it seems to be turning out all right. Though it'll probably scar."

Malcolm chuckled. "Nay matter. It willna be the first."

Her eyes roamed briefly over his chest, stopping here and there at the trails of repaired flesh that peppered his body.

"And won't be the last, I'll wager."

He sighed, letting the breath out slowly. "Nay, probably not the last."

She finished stitching and cleaning the wound but she didn't want to bind it up before he bathed.

"Oh. I suppose we should have let you bathe before I stitched the wound."

"It would ha' been a might easier to clean, but it'll do either way."

"Why didn't you say anything?"

He shrugged. "It didna matter to me one way or the other, and you seemed keen on poking me with that sharp little needle of yours."

"Oh, stop it."

He winked at her and took another drink of whisky. She took the bottle from him, shushing his protests.

"You still have a bath to take and if you're senseless,

you're too big for me to haul out of the tub. You'd just have to drown."

"Och, if ye insist."

"Good. Now be still and let me make sure you aren't injured anywhere else."

With his shirt out of the way and the most grievous wound taken care of, she took her time inspecting him. She let her fingers trail gently across the slope of his shoulders, down his arms, and across his chest, gently prodding for any injury. Her hands slipped lower, across the hard-packed planes of his stomach, stopping at the top of the kilt wrapped about his waist.

His breath was faster, more erratic. As was hers. When her hand slid to his thigh, he reached down and stopped her, covering her hand with his own.

"Ye might want to stop there, lass. Unless ye've decided to explore the benefits of married life after all."

Her gaze shot to his and then back down to where the kilt he wore no longer lay straight across his lap and jumped to her feet, her heart pounding.

"My apologies," she stammered.

He grinned at her. "Nay apologies necessary, lass. That was the best part of my day."

Before she could respond, there was a knock at the door, and she opened it to admit two men carrying a large copper tub followed by Mary and several maids with buckets of steaming water.

She directed them where to set everything up and then closed the door behind them. She turned back around and gasped. Malcolm had dropped his plaid and was stepping into the tub, his body on full display.

He looked back over his shoulder with a wicked grin. "Sorry, lass. I didna wish to waste the hot water."

Her eyes traveled down to the bottom of the foot that

was still outside the tub and back up over every inch of his lean, muscled body. And then he began to turn. She hastily looked away, ignoring his amused laugh.

"Can you bring me the soap and a linen?" he asked.

She risked a glance and let out the breath she'd been holding at the sight of him waist deep in the water. His knees poked out as the tub wasn't nearly large enough for him to stretch out. But he was covered enough she could approach without getting too much of an eyeful.

She tried to putter around the room, cleaning up the remains of her stitching and preparing a bandage for when he was finished. But another surreptitious glance showed him struggling with the linen. He couldn't move much without risking the stitches she'd just done.

She straightened her shoulders and went to him, taking the linen from his hand. "Let me help."

He gazed at her long enough she began to squirm. "There's no need."

"Yes, there is. You'll pull your stitches."

He laughed and sat forward so she could reach his back. "Then I thank ye."

She methodically scrubbed his back, trying to see him as she would a dog who'd been rolling in the mud. The image did nothing to help her. And neither did Malcolm. Every time her hand brushed over him, he tensed. By the time she'd finished washing his arms and chest, both of them were near breathless with the effort. She decided to leave his legs alone. They'd been soaking in the sudsy water. They were clean enough. And if not, he could reach them himself.

"Close your eyes," she said, scooping up water with a bowl.

He obeyed, and she set to work washing his hair. All the tension left him at that, and he let his head go limp on his neck, leaning back so she could knead his scalp and work the soap into his tangled hair. She worked through the knots with her fingers, not stopping until every strand was clean.

She scooped another bowl of water, only this time she forgot to warn him it was coming. The bowl of water dumping on his head startled him so much he flailed, knocking the bowl from her hand and splashing water everywhere.

Sorcha gasped, and then laughed. Malcolm blinked at her, sudsy water streaming down his face looking for all the world like a half drowned cat.

"Funny, is it?"

"Yes," she choked out. He tried wiping the water from his eyes but it only made matters worse and it set her off again. "I'm sorry, but I can't help it." Her laughter pealed out.

"Och, that's no matter." His gentle tone should have warned her, but before she could make a move, his arm snaked out, captured her around the waist, and hauled her into the tub with him.

She gasped and sputtered as the water soaked her. "Malcolm! What are you doing?"

"Ye looked as though ye could use a bit of a bath as well."

"Not with my clothes on!"

They both froze at that. She couldn't believe those words had escaped her lips.

"Well, now, if your clothes are a problem, I'd be happy to help ye remove them."

"I didn't mean…we can't…"

Her hands were braced on his chest and his heart hammered beneath her fingers. Matching the furious beating of her own. His arms came around her waist, pulling her more tightly against him.

"You are my wife," he reminded her.

"I know," she breathed. "But we can't…"

"Why not?"

His head dipped down, and before she could think of

a reason why they couldn't, his lips brushed across hers. So feather-light at first they felt like butterfly wings beating against her skin. Then he kissed her again, pressing his lips to hers. She moaned gently and let her hand slide up around his neck. His hands tangled in her hair, and he turned his head, kissing her again and again until her head spun. He licked gently at her bottom lip and she opened to him, deepening their kiss until she was almost sobbing with need for him.

A brief knock sounded at the door and before either could say anything the door opened and John sauntered inside.

They all froze. John's face broke out in a huge grin.

"I beg yer pardon. I'll um, see myself back out," he said, quickly backing out.

"Bleeding bastard," Malcolm muttered, shocking a laugh out of Sorcha.

She glanced at him but couldn't hold his gaze. She couldn't believe she'd acted so wantonly. Although, he *was* her husband. According to the church and the law and any man, certainly, she was committing a bigger sin by denying him.

She let her hand run down his chest and he sucked in a breath. It took her a moment to realize it had been in pain, not pleasure. And that the liquid on her fingers wasn't water. It was blood.

"Your stitches!" She pushed away from him and pulled herself out of the tub, quickly wringing out her dress as much as she could so she wouldn't soak the rug too much.

"Dinna fash, lass. I'm all right," he insisted.

"No, you aren't. You've torn some stitches. They'll have to be redone."

"Well, I think I had some help."

She froze, heat rushing to her face, and Malcolm laughed. "I enjoyed it, Sorcha."

"You did?" she asked, the sound of her name on his lips sending shivers down her spine.

"Verra much." His voice was deep and husky and made her toes curl in her boots. "Any time ye want to join me in the bath, or anywhere else in this chamber, ye are more than welcome."

She didn't know what to say to that so she kept silent.

"If ye'll hand me a linen, I'll get out of this water and ye can see what can be done about the stitches."

"Oh, yes, here you are." She handed him a folded sheet of soft material and turned before he could step out of the tub, ignoring his soft chuckle.

"It's safe to turn around now," he said, seating himself on a stool before the fire, nothing but the linen wrapped around his waist.

The slight wave of his hair had turned curlier in the water but with the fire at his back it still resembled nothing so much as a lion's mane, framing the face of a proud and regal king. His domain might be nothing more than a crumbling keep, but there was no mistake who ruled it. Her lion stretched a bit, taking care to protect his stitched side, and shook some water droplets from his hair. They fell on his chest and slowly traveled down the planes of his body. Sorcha's mouth went dry at the sight but she tried to focus on the task at hand.

"It's not so bad," she murmured. "Only the one stitch. I think it will be all right if we bandage it well and you try not to exert yourself too much."

"Well, that ruins a few ideas I had in mind."

"What ide—oh," she said, embarrassment flooding her cheeks again, though she refused to look down. She wouldn't act like some simple, innocent virgin, even if that was what she truly was.

She grabbed a length of clean linen to bind the wound, trying to keep her attention on keeping the material straight instead of on the strong body she was applying it to.

"How did this happen, anyway? Sword?"

"Dagger," Malcolm said, grunting a bit when she pulled a little too tight.

"How did someone get close enough to pull a dagger on you?"

Malcolm snorted. "I fell for an old trick. A man lay crumpled in the road. I thought he was a villager and knelt to see if he lived. He jumped up and tried to stab me with his dagger. Proving he was, indeed, verra much alive. But with rotten aim. My good fortune, I suppose, or it would ha' been the last man I attempted to help."

"Who was it? Do you know who attacked the pastures?"

Malcolm was silent long enough that she glanced up from what she was doing to make sure he hadn't fainted dead away. He was conscious, and staring at her with his eyes narrowed in confusion.

"What?" she asked.

"It was Campbell men," he said slowly, like he wasn't sure she'd understand him. "It's always Campbell men."

Chapter Fourteen

Sorcha sat back, denial rising quickly to the surface. "My father would never condone such a thing."

"Whether he condones it or no, I dinna ken. Though I find it hard to believe anything goes on without his knowledge. But the men were most certainly Campbells."

"You can't know that for sure," she insisted, refusing to believe anyone under her father's rule would act in such a manner. "And even if it were a group of Campbells they were probably provoked. My father said he's never sent out a raid party against anyone who didn't deserve it."

Malcolm snorted. "Oh aye, I believe that. The problem is that Angus Campbell believes that anyone who goes against him in any way deserves the harshest punishment. He'll continue to attack my people for the simple sin of existing."

"No," Sorcha said, standing and moving away from him. "You're wrong."

"Look in the bag there," Malcolm said, nodding at a satchel by the door. "Go on."

Sorcha watched him as she moved toward the bag, not

sure if he was trying to trick her or not. "What is in there?"

"The proof of what I'm saying."

She opened the bag, her heart in her throat. Inside was the blood soaked bonnet of a Campbell man. There was no mistaking the design on the brooch buckled to the hat.

She shook her head, unable to accept that truth. "Where is the rest of him?"

"On his way back home, I assume."

"You didn't kill him?"

Malcolm watched her with sad eyes and finally shook his head. "I dinna kill for sport, Sorcha. If there is a man on the other end of my blade, he's there for a verra good reason."

"It was probably in retaliation for all the attacks you've instigated."

"What attacks, Sorcha? I havena been here for more than two months. I've been dancing attendance on the king and yer father at court and then endured yer company for a fortnight."

The word *endure* slashed through her like the dagger blade must have cut through Malcolm. "You needn't worry on that count," she said, folding her arms and removing herself from his immediate vicinity to stand by the fire. The heat of the flames did little to warm the chill that sank into her bones. "I have no desire to force my presence on you any longer than necessary."

"That's no' what I meant…"

"And you haven't been in my despicable presence at all since the moment we arrived at Glenlyon. You left me here and went off with John to do who-knows-what, before I'd even washed the travel dust from my face."

"Aye, but I dinna leave to launch any attacks. I needed to check on my lands and tenants, since I'd been away from them for so long."

"So you say." She ignored the look of blatant anger on his

face. She wasn't even sure she believed what she was accusing him of. She only knew that the alternative could not be true. Her father could not be behind the attacks on the MacGregor villages. Because if he was, then everything she'd been taught her whole life had been a lie.

"Aye," Malcolm said, rising from the stool to tower over her, all the more magnificent in his anger because he wore nothing but a thin linen towel. The faint growl behind his words and the fury in those feline eyes sent a shiver down her spine. "I do say. I may be many things, Sorcha. Not all of them, or even many of them, good. But I am an honorable man. I dinna lie, or cheat, or attack even my enemies, and especially not innocents, without cause. I dinna retaliate against injustice by committing further injustice. Aye, I've attacked yer father's men. But I have only done so in defense of my own, as ye've seen. I dinna ride into villages full of unarmed farmers, women and children, and kill and destroy just to strike at my enemy. Can you, with absolute certainty, say the same about yer father?"

Sorcha searched his face, locked her gaze with his, looked for any hint that he might be deceiving her. That he might be the one instigating this whole war between their clans instead of being the victim. She found nothing.

Yet still… "He is my father."

"Aye. And I'm yer husband. And as we look to be bound together, someday ye'll have to choose who ye are going to believe."

"I know," she said quietly.

She could never choose one without betraying the other. And how was she ever to know who had, or would, betray her? It was impossible.

Exhaustion pulled at her, and she sighed deeply. "I am weary. And I'm certain you must be as well. If you give me your word that you will leave me be, I don't see why we can't share the bed until my chambers are ready. It is certainly large enough."

He watched her for a moment, and then the fire went out of him as well. He gave her a faint smile. "Aye, that it is."

She led the way. Now that the excitement of the bathtub and the horrid argument that followed were behind them, or at least being politely ignored for the time being, the aftermath of being pulled fully clothed into the water finally set in. Sorcha shivered, from cold rather than fear this time, her wet clothing seeming to suck the autumn chill from the air to seep into her bones.

"I must change," she said, expecting Malcolm to politely excuse himself until she'd divested herself of her wet clothing.

"Ye'll need help. Come here."

She spun to face him. "That's quite all right. I can manage on my own."

He shook his head and pulled out his dagger. For a brief moment, panic flared in her breast. She didn't think he'd ever truly threaten her with a weapon but old habits did die hard. She took a step back before she could stop herself.

He pointed at her dress. "Ye'll never get those knots undone now. They'll need to be cut."

"Oh," she said faintly, glancing behind her. He was correct, of course. The ties had gotten wet and swollen. It would take hours to unpick them. "All right then. Cut away."

She turned her back to him and felt a few swift tugs on her boned bodice before her clothing loosened and she could take a truly deep breath for the first time in hours. She held the front of the dress up and hurried into the small dressing room off the main sleeping chamber. She quickly dressed in a thick, warm chemise and pulled on woolen stockings to protect her feet from the chill she couldn't seem to shake, and then hesitantly returned to the bed chamber.

Malcolm had donned a warm sleep shirt and had stoked

the fire in the bedroom fireplace to a cheery crackle. The candles had been extinguished save for the one she held to light her way. With the glow of the fire lending a cozy light, she blew out her candle and set it on the table near her.

Malcolm climbed into bed with a weary sigh and lay back against the bolsters.

"I willna bite, lass, ye have my word," he said.

She smiled at that and climbed into bed. Her stomach still fluttered like a flock of birds had been caged inside, but she did her best to ignore it and scooted beneath the covers. She held herself rigidly on her side of the bed, afraid to move or even breathe too loudly.

After a quarter hour of maintaining the same position, her still-frozen muscles began to cramp and she tried to shift without making too much movement.

"What ails ye, lass?"

She froze, hardly daring to breathe. "Nothing."

"And she accuses me of not being truthful," he muttered, so low she almost didn't hear him. "Come here," he said, reaching over to place a hand on her shoulder. "Jesus, Mary, and Joseph, ye're naught but a block of ice!"

"I'm fine," she insisted, though now that he had pointed out her near freezing state, she couldn't seem to stop the shivers from wracking her body.

"Nay, ye're not. Come here, Sorcha. Now."

He drew her to him, and despite her best intentions to resist, the moment his warm arms wrapped about her she couldn't help but sink in against him with a grateful sigh.

"You're so warm," she said, pressing her frozen nose against his chest.

He yelped a little and then chuckled. "Aye, and it's a good thing, too, or ye'd like to have frozen to death over there. Ye didna say anything. Why?"

"I would have warmed up eventually."

He snorted. "Aye, perhaps, but no' before losing a few toes."

He drew her in tighter against him, wrapping his body around her and tucking the blankets in securely about them. His hands rubbed down her back and arms, over and over until she began to thaw.

"Is that better?" he asked in that husky voice which couldn't help but affect her.

"Much. Thank you."

"'Tis my pleasure," he murmured.

As close to his body as she currently was, she was painfully aware of how much of a pleasure it was for him to hold her. But she couldn't find it in herself to be either scandalized or angry. If anything, she was flattered to affect him so. And more than a little intrigued, though she was certainly too tired and cold to do anything about it.

Now that Sorcha's body was finally beginning to thaw, her exhaustion overwhelmed her. She pressed as close to Malcolm as she could get, and breathed him in, the clean, masculine scent of him filling her senses.

"Do I still reek as though I've been rolling with the pigs in the sty?" he asked.

She giggled. "No. You smell good."

"Oh, aye?" He was obviously surprised. She wasn't sure, but it might have been the first compliment she'd paid him.

"Hmm, yes, you do." Her words were beginning to slur as sleep dragged at her mind. She might regret saying such a thing to him in the morning. But for the moment, she'd never felt so safe and comfortable in her life.

He said something else but she didn't quite catch it. The most she could mumble in return was a garbled, "Hmm?"

He laughed quietly and pressed a tender kiss to her forehead. The last thing she remembered was his soft whisper.

"Sleep well, my wife."

Chapter Fifteen

Malcolm woke the next morning more rested and content than he could remember ever being. His side ached from the dagger's blade but he paid it no mind. He glanced down at the woman still slumbering beside him. She'd fallen asleep tucked up against him, and while he probably should have rolled her to her side of the bed and left her in peace, he'd kept her wrapped in his arms the entire night. She was currently spooned in front of him, her delicious backside snuggled in against his hips. A position that caused a rather interesting problem.

She shifted slightly, wiggling closer to him, and a slight groan escaped his lips. Sorcha's eyes fluttered open and blinked sleepily. He could tell the exact moment when she realized where she was. Her entire body stiffened, frozen in his embrace. But to his surprise, she didn't shout or push him away. After a few moments of lying there, her hand went tentatively to his arm, and rested lightly.

She turned and glanced up at him.

"Hello there," he said.

"Hello." She smiled shyly up at him, and his heart clenched in his chest. She looked adorable cuddled up beside him, her hair tousled from sleep. For the first time, he wondered what it would be like to wake up beside her every morning. He liked the idea. More than he expected. Perhaps, instead of trying to drive her away, he should be trying to win her affections.

Yes, she was a Campbell and still seemed stubbornly loyal to her snake of a father. However, that was only to be expected. And while her loyalty was misguided, it was a credit to her character. If he could show her that he wasn't the enemy her father had portrayed him to be, win her loyalty, perhaps they could build a good life together. He'd like to have a wife he could trust, someone he could turn to, raise children with. He'd been fighting most of his life. A bit of love and peace would be a welcome thing.

"I suppose we should get up and start the day," she said, though he was happy to hear a note of reluctance in her voice.

"Aye," he agreed. "There's much to do today."

"There is?"

"Aye. It's almost Michaelmas. Mrs. Byrd likely already has the house in an uproar with the preparations."

"Oh! I didn't realize. I've never really been part of the preparations before."

"Have ye not? Well, prepare yerself, lass. I'm certain Mrs. Byrd will press ye into service in some way or another. That woman is a tyrant with her celebrations. In fact, we'd best be up before she comes to rouse us from our bed herself."

He leaned over to give her what he intended to be a quick kiss. But the moment his lips met hers, he was lost. Her hand tightened on his arm, and her mouth moved softly under his. She turned in his arms, molding herself to him. He held her closer, drank her in. Explored every corner of her mouth until she clung to him. Aye, she was a fine woman. A match for him in every way. He'd needed such a woman in his life for far too long. And whatever else might be amiss in their relationship, at least with this, they were in tune.

He pressed her against the mattress and settled over her, his hand caressing down her side until he reached her hips. Lightly squeezing her flesh, he rocked against her. She threw her head back and gasped, giving him access to her neck.

He'd barely begun kissing down the slender column of her throat when there was a knock at the chamber door.

Malcolm tore his lips from Sorcha's delectable skin and rested his forehead on her shoulder, his lungs burning for air.

"What is it?" he growled.

Sorcha giggled at his obvious irritation and slapped a hand over her mouth to keep the sound in. He glanced at her, eyebrow raised and a small smile on his lips which only made her giggle more.

"Forgive me, my lord," young Timothy called through the door, "but Mrs. Byrd bid me to ask if ye'd be down presently. She says the men are ready to butcher the sheep and several from the village have come wi' great geese to present to your lairdship and Mrs. Byrd has need of my lady to approve of the decorations and the baking of the *struan* and—"

"Aye, laddie, enough! We'll be down presently."

"The *struan*?" Sorcha asked.

"Och! A Scottish lassie not knowing what a *struan* is? For shame!" he said with a wink.

"A Scottish lassie raised by an English mum, remember. My mother stuck as much to the English traditions as possible."

"It's a very large bannock, usually baked by the eldest daughter of the house using nothing but her hands," he said, taking her hands and kissing each finger.

"Oh," she said, her breath coming quicker with each kiss he bestowed. "Why does she need me for such a task?"

At that, Malcolm hesitated. "I dinna ken, truth be told. I

suppose we should go find out. Before she sends the rest of the household up to disturb our rest."

Sorcha sighed and sat up. "I suppose you're right."

Malcolm got up and quickly dressed, leaning over to kiss her one last time. "I'll see ye below."

Walking out of that room with her still bundled up in his bed went against every instinct Malcolm had. But he didn't want to push things. That morning had been, if he wasn't mistaken, the first time they'd had a conversation without it devolving into a shouting match. Or something thrown at his head. He didn't want to ruin their fragile truce. It was better to leave before one or the other of them said something to cause offense. And besides, he had Michaelmas preparations to see to. Mrs. Byrd usually outdid herself on such occasions. And Malcolm found himself eager to show his new bride Glenlyon all decked out for a celebration.

He hurried down the stairs, whistling a tune under his breath.

• • •

Sorcha stood with Mrs. Byrd in the kitchen, staring down at the mound of flour on a lambskin in front of her. "Are you sure you want me to do this? Isn't it bad luck for the entire household for a whole year if it breaks while it's baking?"

"Och, ye'll do fine, my lady. Besides, it's only bad luck to *you* if it breaks while it's baking."

"Oh? Well, that's…comforting. I suppose."

"'Tis bad luck for the whole household if it breaks after it bakes."

That wasn't nearly as comforting. "Perhaps we should find someone else. Someone who has done this before. I'm not really the eldest daughter of the family."

"But ye are the eldest daughter of yer own father, are ye

not?"

"Well, yes…"

"There we are then. Now, have ye included equal portions of each of the grains we grow on the estate?"

Sorcha nodded. "Yes."

"Good. Now, create a well in the middle…no!"

Sorcha dropped the spoon she'd picked up.

"No spoons. Use your fingers," she said, taking Sorcha's hands and showing her how to make a well in the flour. "There we go. Slowly mix in the sheep's milk." She handed Sorcha the pitcher and she carefully poured it in, mixing with her hand as she went.

"And yer fruit and seeds and a bit o' honey for sweetness." Mrs. Byrd indicated several bowls of dried fruit, and Sorcha chose the cranberries and caraway seeds, remembering Malcom's fondness for them. She took her time kneading the mixture until it formed a smooth, soft dough.

She glanced at Mrs. Byrd who nodded with approval.

"And what do we have here?" Malcolm asked, striding into the room.

"Oh, Malcolm, look!" she said, pulling him over to see the lump of dough she was inordinately fond of.

He chuckled and wrapped his arms around her waist from behind. "Congratulations. It looks mighty tasty. And are those cranberries?" he asked, reaching around her to pluck one out of the dough and pop it in his mouth.

She slapped at his hand. "Yes! Now out with you! The baking is the most difficult part, and I don't want to ruin it. I'll curse the entire household with bad luck."

"Och, I have faith in ye, lass."

"Well, I'm glad one of us does."

He chuckled again and gave her a swift kiss. "The lads and I are off to guard the horses, Mrs. Bryd. I thought I'd see if ye had any morsels to help pass the night?"

"Of course! I ha' baskets all made up for ye just there," she said, indicating several linen covered baskets along a table. "I've put some whisky in there as well, but dinna go getting sloshed and letting the horses get stolen from beneath your noses. Again."

"Perish the thought," Malcolm said with a laugh.

"You'll be out all night guarding the horses?" Sorcha asked, her brow furrowing. "Are they in danger?"

"Aye. Old Gerald has had his eye on my new stallion for months now."

"Old Gerald?" Sorcha tried to remember which of the castle tenants or villagers he might be and finally remembered a wizened old gentleman who spent his days snoring by the fire in the great hall, enjoying his retirement from the forges of the blacksmithy his son and grandsons now ran. Her eyes flew wide in surprise. "How could he possibly steal a horse? And for what reason?"

Everyone laughed and Malcolm hastened to explain. "On the eve of Michaelmas it's permitted to steal yer neighbor's horse, provided it's returned safely by the next evening, of course."

"And why would anyone be inclined to do this?"

"For the races, my lady," young Timothy said.

Sorcha hadn't seen the boy hanging about, but she smiled down at him, fond of the little scamp. "What races would those be?"

"The horse races, my lady. On Michaelmas, everyone goes down to the shores of the loch, and we race the horses."

"Aye, and whoever gets their hands on my stallion will win, no doubt about it. So I aim to guard him well."

Sorcha laughed. "So someone can steal your horse and then use it to win a race against you?"

"I did just such a thing last year," John said, coming in to stand beside Malcolm. "It was a fine race, too."

Malcolm scowled at him, though the grin that accompanied it lessened the effect. "Blackguard."

"The men are gathered, my lord!" someone called in the door.

"Come, lads!" Malcolm said. "We're off!"

Malcolm kissed Sorcha soundly and went off surrounded by the good-natured jibes of his men.

Sorcha laughed at them, then turned back to Mrs. Bryd.

"Now," the older woman instructed, as though they'd never been interrupted, "tear a small piece of dough off and throw it into the fire. Must always remember to make your offering to keep the Evil One away."

Sorcha did as instructed and then took the bowl of batter made from cream, eggs, and butter that Mrs. Byrd handed to her. "Brush the batter over it with the cockerel feather, and when it turns a golden brown ye'll turn it and add more batter."

Sorcha took a deep breath. As Mrs. Byrd had explained it to her, this was the most important part. Keeping the cake from burning ensured good or bad luck for her and the household. She'd worked hard so the people of Glenlyon would accept her, especially as they had no reason to do so with her being a Campbell. Truth to tell, they'd been much more welcoming than she'd expected. More welcoming than her own clan would have been to a MacGregor, that's for certain.

They were good people. And working for them and caring for them had given her a sense of purpose and fulfillment she'd been missing her whole life. She'd never thought it possible, but she was beginning to think she might be truly happy at Glenlyon. The last thing she wanted to do as a newcomer was to ruin one of their traditions and bring bad luck down on the house.

She carefully spread the batter on the cake with the

feather, not the easiest of tasks even if it was sturdy, as feathers went. Then she carefully turned the cake to bake on the special stone that the men had brought up from the loch and set before the fire especially for this occasion.

She repeated this until there were three layers on each side of the cake. Finally, Mrs. Bryd declared the struan done and Sorcha removed it from the cooking stone and transferred it to the table to cool.

"It didn't break!" she said with a huge grin. Baking a cake was a small thing, not something that she'd have even deigned to do even a few months ago. But completing the task and doing well filled Sorcha with a pride she hadn't experienced in quite some time. Pride in a job well done and in being part of something that would bring joy to so many.

This particular cake would be for the family, and others would be made for the rest of those who would be dining at the castle the next day. And suddenly, Sorcha could not wait for the celebration.

She swept the leftover flour on the lambskin into a small pile, and Mrs. Byrd handed her a stocking to gather it into.

"There," Mrs. Bryd said, tying a deft knot in the top of the sock. "We'll save this for Himself to take down to sprinkle on the sheep and land in the morning for the blessing. It never fails to bring us a plentiful crop and good fortune for the next year."

"Truly?"

"Truly. Why, look at the good fortune we've already had! The laird bringing home such a beautiful lady as wife," she said, giving Sorcha's arm a pat. "And who knows, mayhap soon we'll be blessed with a few wee bairns to spoil as well." She gave Sorcha a motherly smile and bustled off to see to the gingerbread that was baking in the oven and filling the kitchen with a smell so heavenly Sorcha's mouth watered.

Children. With her blue eyes and Malcolm's flaming hair.

Sorcha found herself smiling at the thought before she could catch it and talk some sense into herself.

They celebrated Michaelmas in England as well, but not in such a personal manner. It had been an occasion to feast and dance and show off her newest gown. Not for giving thanks for a good harvest and to bless the inhabitants of the estate for the coming year. She found she truly enjoyed the intimate traditions and feeling of community at Castle Glenlyon.

A few young women came in with baskets of carrots they'd harvested as gifts for their sweethearts and bobbed quickly to her with happy smiles as they hurried off to do their work. Their easy acceptance of her presence brought a lump to her throat, and she rubbed a hand across her eyes to rid them of any telltale moisture.

"Och! Now whatever is the matter, my lady?" Mrs. Bryd said.

Sorcha glanced up, embarrassed to be caught feeling so sentimental.

"It's nothing, truly. Only I…I suppose I hadn't expected to feel happy here, or welcomed."

"But of course ye'd be welcome and shame to whoever said otherwise. Why wouldna ye be?"

"I thought my name alone would be enough to condemn me."

"Och," Mrs. Bryd waved that away. "Names change. It's the person behind them that counts."

"Even with all the trouble that's been between our clans?"

"Well, there has been a good bit o' that, to be sure. I'll admit there may ha' been a touch of ditherin' to hear the laird had taken a Campbell bride. But the laird's wife ye are. That's enough for most of us. And those who may have had pause have surely changed their minds since meeting ye. Why, anyone can see what a kind and caring lady ye are, taking such good care of all the Glenlyon folk. Ye've won over even the most stubborn, I daresay. And I see how happy ye make his lairdship. That's more than enough for me."

Sorcha blinked up in surprise. "I make him happy?"

"Of course ye do! Didna ye see him in here not a few moments ago? Smiling and carrying on as though he were a carefree lad again. It does me good to see him so." Mrs. Byrd dashed a hand under her own suddenly moist eyes. "That poor man has had a hard time of it, truth be told. His poor sainted mother dead of a fever when he was but a lad. And then his father and brother being killed in one of these never ending raids and leaving him alone to handle all this." She shook her head. "It was more than any young man should have to bear, and that's the truth. But the laird has done well. He's a good master. He deserves some happiness in his life. I'm glad he's finally found some," she said, giving Sorcha a pat on the cheek.

Sorcha went about the rest of the preparations in a bit of a daze and lay in bed late into the night, thinking about Malcolm with his men in the stables, watching over the horses. Surely a man who inspired such loyalty and love couldn't be the monster her father had always portrayed him. Hadn't she seen that for herself? In the tender way he held her, in the passion behind his kisses? Even during their most heated rows, he had often taken his lead from her, lashed out when she did, not the other way around, even though she'd given him more than enough cause. And through it all, he'd watched over her, protected her, seen that she was cared for, whether she deserved it or not.

She couldn't stop thinking about his arms about her, his lips on her skin, and how it might be if she became his wife in truth. It might be too much to dare hope, but perhaps, if they both put away their prejudices, they could build a life together.

For the first time, she didn't want to consider how her

father might feel about it. How it might affect him. The king had been right—the raids needed to end. Too much had been lost over the centuries that the clans had been rivals. If her marriage to Malcolm could end all that, why should she fight against it? Even if he'd been an old, loathsome tyrant. And he was far from that.

On the contrary, her husband was young, strong, and so handsome her heart near jumped from her chest every time he walked in a room. The Lion, they called him. And with good reason. Proud, regal, fierce. And now that she'd gotten to know him better, she knew precisely how stubborn he could be. She'd never drive him away. So perhaps she should seize what happiness she could find. And try, instead, to win his love.

A fierce excitement rushed through her, and Sorcha flopped over on her side so she could smother her smile in Malcolm's pillow. Tomorrow Malcolm would find himself married to a very different wife. She just prayed he'd like her.

Chapter Sixteen

Sorcha stood with the other women near the shore of the loch, and raised her hand to shield her eyes from the sun. Despite Malcolm's best efforts, Old Gerald had, in fact, managed to steal his stallion, and Malcolm was at that moment giving Gerald a few tips on how to ride the enormous animal.

Malcolm clapped Gerald on the back and turned to mount the horse he'd be riding that day. But it wasn't the horse that had Sorcha's attention. She sat back, her breath catching in her throat at the sight of her husband. He rode toward her, his plaid flapping out behind him. He sat astride the horse effortlessly. Though his hand held the reins, he scarce seemed to need them. He could probably control the animal through nothing but the grip of his strong, bare thighs that his kilt did nothing to hide. He exuded strength and power in a way she'd never seen a man do before. Not even the king.

Just as he reached her, the sun broke through the clouds, illuminating his fiery mane like a halo. He stopped beside their group and crooked his finger at her, a heart-stopping smile on his lips. The other women giggled behind their hands.

Sorcha ignored them and went to him, craning her neck so she could speak to him.

"You summoned me, my lord?" she asked, giving him a half smile.

"Are ye ready?" he asked, reaching out a hand.

"Are you sure this is necessary?"

"It's such fun, my lady! It's custom," Mary said. She was mounted behind one of the lads Sorcha had seen working in the stables.

Sorcha couldn't help but smile. All around her, the women were mounting up behind their men and lining up at the start line.

She took a deep breath and clasped Malcolm's arm. He hauled her up behind him, and she wrapped her arms tightly about his waist. "What if I fall?"

"I hope ye do," he said, bringing his horse into line beside the others.

"What?" *So this is his revenge? Death by horse?*

"Oh, aye, milady," Mary chimed in. "It's great luck if the woman falls during the race."

Sorcha frowned. "Well, that seems a bit odd. Are you sure—"

"Hold tight now, lass!" Malcolm said, patting her arms where they gripped his waist.

At a signal from someone up ahead, the horses bolted amidst great whoops and hollers from both the riders and the spectators on the shore. Sorcha tucked her head down against Malcolm's back and held on for all the she was worth.

All went well for the first few paces. And then the jolting of the running horse loosened her grip on Malcolm.

"There goes the first one!" Malcolm called back to her.

She risked a glance around his shoulder and saw a woman tumbling on the beach. She jumped up and waved, to the cheers of the others.

Sorcha's teeth rattled from the rhythm of the horse beneath her, and her fingers slipped a fraction more.

"Malcolm!" she shouted. But it was too late. Her hold slipped and off she tumbled onto the banks of the loch.

"Sorcha!"

Malcolm reined in his horse and twisted in his saddle but Sorcha waved him on. He smiled and spurred his horse on to make up lost ground.

The icy loch water splashed against her, soaking into her skirts. She shoved away the damp tendrils of hair that trailed across her face and glanced up to see the village women surrounding her, faces alight with joy and celebration.

They hauled her out of the water, wrapped a plaid about her shoulders, and led her up the bank, all the while giving their congratulations on the luck she was sure to have. Why falling off a horse was good luck, she couldn't fathom. She grimaced and rubbed her bruised and aching backside. Other than that minor injury, she seemed whole and hearty. And thoroughly soaked.

"Oh! The laird is winning, my lady!" one of the women called, and they all hurried up the bank to catch the end of the race.

She could just make out Malcolm, hunched over the saddle. He'd somehow made up the distance he'd lost and in a sudden burst of speed managed to cross over the finish line a horse head before Old Gerald.

The rest of the horses crossed, and the ensuing moments were a whirl of cheers, congratulations, and good-natured jokes as friends and neighbors debated the merits of horses and riders.

Malcolm nudged his horse through the onlookers and trotted back to Sorcha's side, dismounting the moment he reached her.

"Are ye all right?" he asked her, pulling her into his arms.

She went gratefully. Whatever their differences, at the moment, he was warm and big enough to block the cool wind that blew off the loch. He wrapped his arms tighter about her and her shivering lessened a bit.

"I'm fine. Just wet. And cold. And..." she shifted again, another ache going through her bottom, "a little sore."

"Oh?" Malcolm's hand slipped down and he grabbed a handful of the offending flesh. "Shall I work out the stiffness for ye?"

"Malcolm!" she said, pushing away from him and glancing about to see if anyone had seen what he'd done.

If the laughing nudges and winks were any indication, everyone had.

"You're terrible," she said, trying to glare, though it was impossible to be sour with everyone in such a good mood.

"I was merely trying to ease yer discomfort."

"*Mm-hmm.* Well, I'll thank you to leave my...*discomfort* alone."

He laughed and pulled her back under his arm, flinging his plaid over her shoulders for more protection.

"Come on, wife. We must distribute the prizes. And then we can get ye out of those wet clothes."

"We?"

"I am ever at yer service, madam."

The rush of heat that burned through her at the thought of what those services might include brought a coy smile to her lips she didn't attempt to hide. Malcolm saw it and gave a mock growl, hugging her tighter. "If we didna have half the castle waiting for us..."

"Yes, well, we do."

His disappointed sigh had Sorcha laughing with gratified amusement as they rejoined their people. Malcolm brought her to an area that had been cleared, and he proceeded to call up the winners from each of the races of the day. Sorcha, as lady of the keep, handed out the baskets of goodies and small bags of coins to the winners, and presented each person who came in second with a kiss on the cheek, much to the delight of all.

When it came time to claim his own prize as winner of the last race, Malcolm held up his hands to quiet the cheering. Sorcha glanced at him, eyebrows raised in question.

"I propose a trade, Gerald! I find that as magnificent as the winning prize is," he said gesturing to the beautiful carved antler cup Sorcha held, "the only prize I wish to claim is a kiss from the beautiful lady of Glenlyon."

Cheers erupted from the gathered crowd, and Gerald good-naturedly bowed and accepted the antler from his lady.

"You'd really rather a kiss than a prize, my lord?" Sorcha asked, her heart thudding in her chest.

He wrapped his arms about her and held her against him, high enough her feet dangled off the ground. "From the most beautiful lady in Scotland? What prize could be greater?"

She laughed, and before she could say another word, he kissed her. She expected a quick peck on the lips but Malcolm was having none of that. His lips claimed hers and her embarrassment at having an audience quickly disappeared under his onslaught. He didn't release her until she was breathless, light-headed, and heartily wishing they were alone in their bedchamber.

He gave her a final quick kiss and then bowed to her. "My thanks, lady."

She curtsied back. "My pleasure, my lord."

His eyebrow raised, and she gave him a slow, smoldering smile that sparked an answering heat in his eyes. The crowd, it seemed, enjoyed her response as well, and they once again cheered.

Malcolm helped her mount up behind him again and led the procession to the church for the circuiting. Everyone rode around the building and churchyard three times sunwise, visiting their buried ancestors in a tradition so old no one remembered when it had started. Sorcha had never seen anything like it before, but it was done with a reverence and comfort that showed just how important the old customs were to these people.

In fact, the entire day had held customs that had been practiced for longer than anyone could remember and she loved being a part of it all. Joining in the celebrations and taking part in the traditions with them filled Sorcha with a sense of rightness like nothing else she'd ever experienced. She'd never felt such belonging—not just to a place, but to a people. She'd expected to have to live in Glenlyon. She'd never expected that it would feel like home. But, she truly felt as if she were one of them now. Accepted. Wanted. Kin.

She snuggled into Malcolm, smiling when he leaned back into her and pulled her even closer. She let out a happy sigh.

Home.

. . .

Sorcha wrapped another garland around the column, smiling to herself at the beautiful arrangement. She'd arranged flowers before, of course, but she'd never supervised such a grand undertaking as this, let alone taken such an active part in the actual preparations. She was enjoying herself more than she thought she would. Except for the constant fear that she'd make a horrible mistake and ruin the entire celebration.

"Oh, my lady, that's so lovely!" Mary exclaimed, hurrying over with another armful of autumn foliage.

"Thank you. I wasn't sure how it's normally done, but I thought perhaps it would look nice."

"It's beautiful, my lady, truly. And here is more!" she said, dropping her load on the dais near the table.

"Oh goodness," Sorcha said with a laugh. "I do believe Mrs. Byrd will have every square inch of this place covered before too long."

As she spoke, a few white petals fluttered down in front of her face and Sorcha batted them away, only to have more take their place, raining down on her head. She glanced up to see Malcolm standing on the rafters above her head.

He smiled and waved down at her.

"What are you doing up there?" she called up, her heart suddenly in her throat.

"Draping more of this infernal bunting," he said, holding up the end of the same material they'd draped across the tables.

"Come down from there at once! You'll rip out your stitches again."

"Och, dinna fash. I'll be fine."

John came to stand beside her, and she tried appealing to him instead, since her husband had obviously addled his brains.

"Dinna fash, he says. After I spend half the night stitching him closed not even two nights ago. Can't you talk any sense into him?"

He laughed. "Not likely. He doesna have two licks of sense between his ears. He's probably fine, though. He's as nimble as a cat."

"Even cats fall occasionally."

"Aye," Malcolm called from up above. Then he grabbed the rope dangling from the beam and jumped. As he came down, the bunting rose, draping across the beam perfectly. Sorcha covered her face with her hands until she heard the soft thump of Malcolm landing beside her.

"But we always land on our feet," he said, wrapping an arm around her waist and pulling her in for a quick kiss.

"Oh!" She slapped at his arm. "You'll turn all my hair

white with fright if you keep up that nonsense."

"Ye'd look beautiful with yer hair all white. Like an angel," he said, drawing her close. He leaned in so only she could hear him. "I didna think ye cared so much, my lady."

She looked up at him, her heart nearly strangling her. "I didn't think so either."

He blinked, surprised. "Changed yer mind, have ye?"

"Aye, laddie," she said, trying to match his brogue and draw a smile from his lips. "I think perhaps I have." She forced herself to meet his eyes. "As the king saw fit to give me a husband, I thought perhaps I'd try to be a wife. If that's something which interests you."

His eyes searched hers and she wasn't sure if he was trying to determine if she meant what she said or if he was trying to find the least, or perhaps most, insulting way to decline her offer of a truce.

As each second ticked by, her heart pounded harder, so loudly she thought he'd surely hear it.

Finally, he took a deep breath and reached a hand up to cup her face, his thumb lightly caressing her skin.

"I'd like nothing more, *mo chridhe*."

His heart? The sound of that on his lips had her own about to burst with hope and joy.

He leaned down and pressed a gentle kiss to her lips. Then he rested his forehead against hers and drew in a deep breath, as if she were the very air he breathed.

"I've never resented a celebration more than I do right now," he murmured and she pulled back enough to look into his eyes.

"Why is that?" Worry snaked through her that she'd done something wrong to ruin things after all.

He pulled her closer. "Because if I didna have work to do, I'd carry ye to our bedchamber and explore yer newfound willingness to be my wife."

Her heart leapt and her stomach flipped, making her both light-headed and slightly nauseous, and simultaneously hot and cold. It seemed she was just as eager as he.

"I do not wish to dissuade you from performing your husbandly duties," she said with as sly of a smile as she could muster, "but I've never worked so hard in my life and if you dare delay this celebration, I can't be held responsible for what I do."

He released her with a laugh and a little bow. "As my lady desires. I give ye my word, the celebration shall occur right on schedule."

"My lady," Timothy said, running up to her. "All your things have arrived!"

"My things?" she looked at Malcolm. "Oh! My trunks, all my belongings. Thank you, Timothy," she said, leaning down to give him a big hug.

He squirmed away and ran off. Sorcha smiled, happy that her things had arrived just before the celebration. She found, to her surprise, that she wasn't nearly as excited to be in possession of all her gowns and trapments as she had once been. The homespun dresses she'd been wearing were much more suited for the simpler country life. Her elaborate court dresses would be out of place here. But perhaps she'd find occasion for them at some point. And she'd definitely be able to find some lovely ribbons and laces among her trunks to use as gifts for Mrs. Bryd and Mary and the village women who had befriended her.

Malcolm called over one of the men. "Take the trunks that have arrived up to Lady Glenlyon's chambers."

The man nodded and scurried off to do his laird's bidding.

Sorcha looked at Malcolm, trying to determine what he might be thinking. After what they'd said…

He wrapped an arm about her again and whispered into her ear. "I seem to remember a veritable fortress of trunks that we'd left behind. With all those trunks occupying your chamber, I'm afraid ye'll have to continue to stay in mine for the time being."

"Is that so?" she asked, smiling up at him.

"*Hmmm*, I didna think ye'd have any objections."

"Well, there you go thinking again. You know, it's really not one of your better abilities."

"Oh? And what would those abilities be?"

Her cheeks grew warm but before she could answer someone cleared her throat and Sorcha tore her gaze from Malcolm to look behind them.

"My lady," Berta said, dropping into a short curtsy.

"Berta!" Sorcha untangled herself from Malcolm and swept her maid up in a hug. "How are you? How was the journey? You must be tired."

Berta glanced back and forth between her and Malcolm and then seemed to remember herself. "Oh, the journey was uneventful, my lady. Though long. I am happy to have finally arrived. I've been worried about how you've been managing here…all alone." She gave Malcolm another look.

"Oh, I've been managing fine."

At Berta's startled and slightly hurt, puckered expression, Sorcha hastily added, "I've missed you terribly, of course. But Mary has been taking great care of me." She gestured to Mary who was hurrying past with her arms full of greenery. She stopped when she heard her name and gave Sorcha a quick little bob.

Sorcha smiled at her and waved her on her way. "They have truly been very welcoming here. Much more than I would have expected."

"So it would seem," Berta said, though she still looked around her as though she expected an army of warriors to jump out at her. "Well, in any case, I've brought all your things with me so we can get you properly attired again…"

She eyed the simple dress that Sorcha wore, her nose wrinkling in disapproval at its plainness.

"And your father, of course, has sent some gifts."

"How lovely of him. And I'm happy to have my things, naturally. Though we don't stand on ceremony here. Except on special occasions."

Berta's eyes widened slightly in surprise and did another perusal of Sorcha's gown.

"I was helping decorate for the Michaelmas celebration banquet tonight. Oh! How wonderful, you've come just in time," she said, clapping her hands as she remembered the reason they had stripped the entire countryside to decorate the hall. "We've been preparing for days and the kitchen is full of the most delicious things."

She chattered away to Berta about the *struan Michael* and everything they had planned as she led her to her newly finished chambers and showed her the small room off the side of her own that was kept for her personal maid's use.

"It sounds as though you have been kept very busy, my lady," Berta said, her tone indicating more disapproval than interest.

"Yes. Well, there is always something to do on an estate of this size."

As soon as the men had brought in the last box and left Berta turned to Sorcha. "I thought they'd never leave. Oh, my lady, are you well? Truly? Has it been dreadful?"

Sorcha blinked at her maid in total confusion until she realized that when they'd last seen each other Sorcha had been certain she was on her way to her doom. She hurried to reassure her.

"I'm perfectly well, Berta. Do I look ill or mistreated?"

"Well, no, my lady. But…"

"I think…I think I may have been wrong about the MacGregors. At least Malcolm and the people here. They have treated me with nothing but kindness and respect and even Malcolm himself…well…"

"Yes." Berta sniffed disdainfully. "I can see. Have you changed your mind then? Do you no longer wish to escape from this marriage?"

Sorcha paused long enough that Berta's eyes widened in shock. "You would truly wish to remain here as a MacGregor captive, rather than return to your own clan?"

Sorcha gave a stilted laugh. "I'm not held captive, Berta. I am the lady here. The wife of the laird and treated with as much regard as that title affords me. A great deal more, actually. And Lord Glenlyon, while he has his faults—many, many faults—he has, for the most part, treated me well. Or at least no worse than I treated him. We've come to an agreement recently…"

Her cheeks flamed remembering exactly how they'd reached their agreement.

Berta's frown deepened. "And what of the raids and crimes they've committed against your kinsman?"

Sorcha sighed. "I'm not sure what I believe. The people I've come to know, even Malcolm…I don't think they are capable of the things we've always heard."

"So they haven't ridden out at all? There have been no raids or skirmishes?"

"Well, yes, there was. But Malcolm and his men didn't instigate it. They encountered Campbell men on our lands and had to rout them."

"Perhaps. Or perhaps their purpose was to attack Campbell men and they only told you what they wanted you to believe."

Sorcha frowned. "I was here when they came back. They even brought several men from the village who had been wounded defending their flocks."

"So they say."

"I was here, Berta…"

"Yes, but you weren't *there*. And even if, as you say, Campbell men attacked first, it was most likely in retaliation for a previous attack."

Sorcha's frown deepened. There had been that one week where Malcolm and John had left, just after arriving at Glenlyon. Still, Malcolm's insistence that they wouldn't attack unarmed villagers when that is precisely what happened to Glenlyon's village rankled her. Even if that attack *had* been provoked, why attack the innocent villagers? Unless Malcolm had attacked a Campbell settlement first.

"My apologies, my lady, for speaking so openly. But I worry for you. I think it would be wise to remember that these are MacGregors and despite your marriage, you are a Campbell. Do you really believe they would tell you if it had been them who had struck first? Or would they tell you they'd only acted in defense against an attack?"

"But Malcolm and John were here at the keep when the raid occurred. They couldn't have been leading it."

Berta waved that away. "They could have ordered it done, easily enough."

Sorcha couldn't answer that. Her gut reaction was to insist Malcolm wouldn't lie to her. Quite the opposite, in fact. He really seemed to enjoy throwing the truth in her face. But in this situation, with their clans fighting against each other? Would he tell her if he was striking first? She didn't know. Would she tell him if their positions were reversed?

"I can see I've upset you, my lady. That was not my intent."

"No, no. I'm all right. I…have a lot on my mind."

Berta nodded. "Of course." Then she pulled a sealed letter out of her cloak pocket. "From your father. He instructed that it be given to you right away, but I thought it prudent to wait until we were alone."

Sorcha bit her tongue to keep from snapping that they

were safe and dismissed Berta to go freshen up. She carried her letter to the fire and broke the seal. Her father didn't waste time on niceities, somehow dutifully asking after her well being while simultaneously chastising her for not doing his bidding and failing to contact him. He was eager to hear of her new home and family.

She found his interest in her day-to-day life suspicious. He'd never shown much of an interest in how she'd spent her days before. Did he merely wish to ensure his only daughter was content in her new life, as he said? Or was he perhaps hoping to glean details of his enemy's stronghold and whereabouts? For what purpose Sorcha could easily imagine.

She tossed the letter into the fire before she could change her mind. He'd get no such information from her. She would, however, write immediately and tell him of her contentment. Ask him to stop the raids. Explain that Malcolm truly had no desire to continue their feud. Whether he liked it or no, she was now a MacGregor. And she had every intention of embracing her new clan, and her new life as the lady of Glenlyon.

Hopefully, he'd understand and accept it. If he didn't… well, she'd be too far away to deal with him. And Malcolm would be here if she needed protection. Of that, at least, she could be certain. He'd sworn she'd come to no harm and would keep his word. Maybe someday she would be more than a matter of honor to him. Perhaps she already was. He'd called her his heart, and he wasn't a man to use such a term lightly. In the meantime, she'd make sure she did nothing to worsen their relationship. Until she could find a way to strengthen it.

Chapter Seventeen

Malcolm watched as Sorcha read the letter he assumed to be from her father and then tossed it in the fire. After several minutes spent scribbling back a reply, she summoned a page and gave orders for the letter to be sent immediately.

What was so urgent? And so private she needed to burn the letter upon reading? *Only one way to find out...*

He walked into the room, and Sorcha raised startled eyes to him. His gaze shifted to the fire.

"Sorcha," he said, not accusing her of anything. Yet. He was curious to see how she'd react to being caught in the act.

"Malcolm." She came toward him with a slight smile, strain visible in the taut lines of her body. She followed his gaze to the fire. "My father," she said, with a slight shrug.

He raised a brow. "You burned a letter from yer father?" At her nod, he continued. "Why would ye feel the need to do that?"

She sighed deeply. "My temper got the better of me, I suppose. My father didn't just agree to this marriage to appease the king. I believe he thought to take advantage of the situation, as we were forced into it, anyway."

"He wanted you to spy for him."

"He never said so in so many words, but I believe so, yes."

Of course. He'd been so stupid. "Ah. And have ye followed his wishes?"

He stood a scant few inches from her. Close enough to reach out and take her in his arms. Yet, he had to know.

"No," she said, her chin raised in defiance. Putting on her brave face.

"And the messenger?"

She sucked in a quick breath, her eyes widening. She hadn't known he'd seen the messenger.

"I sent a reply. Telling him I was happy in my new home."

Now it was his turn to be surprised. "Ye are happy here?"

"Yes." She came to him and wrapped her arms about his waist. "I didn't think I would be, but somehow, I am."

He drew her in, taking her chin in his fingers to lift her face.

"He'll have to find a spy somewhere else," she said, rising on her toes to reach him.

Their lips met and fused together. A tiny moan came from her, and he crushed her to him, ravenous for her. She, it seemed, felt the same. She looped her arms about his neck, digging her hands into his hair to keep him locked against her. Not that he had any intention of trying to escape.

"My lord, my lord!" a small voice came from outside the door.

Malcolm groaned and released her. He stalked to the door and jerked it open. "Tell Mrs. Byrd we'll be right down, Tim."

"Aye, milord!"

Timothy scampered out of sight, and Sorcha giggled. Malcolm glanced at her over his shoulder. With her flushed cheeks and lips swollen from his kisses, his wife presented an altogether too-tempting picture. He stepped out of their chamber before he gave in to that temptation, Michaelmas celebration be damned.

"It seems our presence is needed below," he said. "Will ye come?"

"Of course. I just need a moment."

"Don't be too long."

She rolled her eyes and shooed him away, and Malcolm went to join in the celebration with a heart lighter than it had been in years. He pushed aside any niggling doubts he might have. He'd found a harmony with his wife he'd never dreamed possible. He wouldn't let anything ruin it.

At least for tonight.

Malcolm hadn't been able to tear his eyes from his wife all evening. She'd eaten, danced, and made merry with his people, but there was an air of anxiety about her that sent a qualm of unease through him. Had it to do with her sour-faced maid? The woman had only stayed at the celebration long enough to eat and then disappeared, pleading exhaustion. While Malcolm was glad to be rid of her, he didn't trust the wholly Campbell creature. Nor did he like what influence she might have on Sorcha. He'd allow nothing to ruin the new understanding they seemed to have found. He only hoped Sorcha's seeming nervousness wasn't on account of any new trouble the Campbell clan was stirring.

Enough of this. He was going to enjoy the evening. He drained his glass and left the table, moving through the crowd to join Sorcha where she stood surrounded by his people. A burst of warmth rushed through him at the sight of his wife laughing and talking as though she'd been a part of his clan her whole life.

She glanced up when he approached, and her face lit up with a smile that erased any lingering doubts he had. He took her hand.

"Come with me."

"Where are we going?" she said, though she followed readily enough.

He led her to a corner by the hearth where it was a little less crowded and opened his sporran, taking out the delicately embroidered purse he'd purchased for her from the village earlier that day.

"I wanted to present ye with yer Michaelmas gifts," he said, handing it to her with more trepidation than he expected. He found he very much hoped she'd like what he'd chosen for her.

"Oh, Malcolm. This is beautiful!" Her fingers ran lightly over the brightly patterned thistles and knots. She looked up, her face alight with happiness. "Thank you so much."

"I'm pleased ye like it," he said. "I've one more for ye."

This time she looked down and gasped. And then burst out laughing. He grinned. "Since ye misplaced the one ye used on our wedding night," he said, handing her the dagger.

She took it and carefully drew the dainty blade from its sheath of patterned leather.

"It's but a wee thing, but it'll do the job right enough. Its size is better suited to yer smaller hand."

One dark brow rose and she smiled and slid the blade home again. "It's absolutely perfect, Malcolm. Thank you."

She rose on tip toe and pressed a kiss to his cheek. He smiled down at her, more pleased than he could have hoped.

"I have some gifts for you as well," she said, her cheeks flushing pink.

"Do ye now?" he asked, the happy surprise evident in his voice.

She pulled a pair of deep blue garters from her pocket,

and he took them with pleasure.

"They are grand, Sorcha, I thank ye. Not quite so grand as those bonnie blue eyes of yours," he said, drawing a finger gently down her cheek. "But verra close."

She gave him a nervous smile and bit her lip. All around them, couples were exchanging similar gifts and the hall was filled with happy laughter. But Malcolm's attention was all for his wife. He waited for her to summon the courage to say what she obviously wanted to say.

She pulled out another bag and handed it to him, taking a deep breath. Her next words stole the wind from his own lungs.

"Ruth agus rath air do iaighe 's eirigh."

He stared at her a moment, and then opened the *crioslachain* bag. He knew what he'd find inside, but the surprise rippling through him at her knowledge of their ancient custom still had him dumbfounded. Her words— "progeny and prosperity on thy lying a rising"—the blessing a woman gave to her beloved as she presented him with a token harvest, echoed through his mind.

He pulled out the bunch of wild carrots, picked with her own hand, his happiness doubling when he saw the large forked carrot amongst them. Luck. For them. For their marriage. For their progeny.

She waited expectantly, her small teeth biting her lower lip. He put the carrots back in the bag and tucked it into his sporran. Then he took her chin between his fingers and gently kissed her.

"Piseach agus pais air an lamh a thug," he said.

He kissed her again.

"Por agus pais dha mo ghradh a thug."

And again.

"Piseach agus pailteas gun an airc na d'chomhnuidh."

She sighed, her eyes fluttering closed.

"Banas agus brioghas dha mo nighinn duinn. Baireas agus buaidh dha mo luaidh a thug."

He kissed her slowly, gently cradling her face in his hands. When he finally released her, she smiled shyly up at him.

"Mary taught me the words to say, and said you might respond in kind. But she didn't tell me what your words would mean."

Malcolm smiled and brushed a thumb across her bottom lip. "It's a blessing for a man's beloved. Progeny and peace on the hand that gave." He took her hand and pressed a kiss to her open palm. "Issue and peace on my love who gave. Progeny and plenty without scarcity in thy dwelling. Wifehood and motherhood on my brown maid." He caressed her dark hair and kissed her forehead. "Endowment and prosperity to my love who gave."

Her breath released in a tremulous sigh. "Prosperity and plenty sound lovely."

"Aye," he said with a smile.

"And peace."

"Peace," he repeated, drawing her closer. "Aye, peace would indeed be a blessing."

"Yes, it would."

"Sorcha," he said, her name a whisper on his lips.

Her gaze dropped, and her breaths came quicker. "Wifehood…"

"Aye?" He wrapped her in his arms, not daring to hope.

"I think…I think I would very much like to be a wife, Malcolm. If you'd like to be my husband."

A bolt of sheer joy blazed through him and he scooped her up in his arms, marching out of the great hall, up the stairs, and into his bedchamber, not stopping until he kicked the door closed behind him with a solid thump. He slowly lowered her feet to the floor and kissed down the column of her throat as he turned her around to reach her laces. She helped as she could, stepping from the gown and petticoats and turning to reach for him again with impatience.

He kissed her, so lost in the sweet taste of her lips he could scarcely think straight. But he tore his mouth from hers, wanting there to be no mistake. He'd not have what was about to happen come back to haunt him later.

"Are ye sure this is what ye want, Sorcha? To be my wife, in truth?"

She blinked up at him, her lips swollen with his kisses, her eyes dark with passion. She gave him a crooked little smile and reached up to run her fingers through his hair.

"Aye, *mo leòmhann*. Make me yours."

Her lion, eh? He smiled back and gathered her to him with a growl. Well, if he was her lion, she was every inch his lioness. Sleek, beautiful, cunning. His perfect match. And he'd happily spend the rest of their lives showing her just how perfect a match they were. Starting right then.

• • •

Sorcha gasped when Malcolm pulled her to him, the almost primal growl deep in his throat spurring an answer within her. But instead of the instant ravishing she expected, he nuzzled gently at her neck. His lips trailed up the tender skin, raising goose flesh in their wake.

"Malcolm," she breathed.

"I want to see ye," he murmured, setting her from him enough so he could push the sleeves of her chemise from her shoulders.

She shivered, both from the chill of the room and the heat of his eyes, but she stood proudly and let her husband gaze upon her.

"You are more beautiful than I ever dreamed." He came to her, leaning down to press a tender kiss to her lips.

"And will you repay the favor?" she asked, though her furiously beating heart had the words coming out fainter than she'd hoped.

"If ye wish," he said, his eyes burning into hers.

He removed his boots and stockings and released the buckle on his belt, letting it, and his kilt, drop to the floor. He stood before her in nothing but his shirt. Which was far too much. She came to him, keeping her eyes locked with his, and slipped her hands beneath his shirt. She pushed up, letting her hands trail up his thighs and run over the cords of his hips, bringing the fabric up with her as she went. Inch by inch he was revealed. She'd seen his naked chest before, of course. But somehow, it seemed much different this time.

She leaned forward and kissed the hard plane of his chest. He sucked in a breath. She glanced up at him and he yanked his shirt over his head in one smooth motion. She had a moment of breath-halting awe beholding him in his full glory. Every inch of him looked the part of a battle-hardened warrior. From the muscles, solid with strength, and the scars that lined his body to the way he held himself, proud, fearless, and ready to pounce. The halo of his hair framed the face that had become beloved to her. With those beautiful, predator eyes. Eyes that hungered for her.

She closed the distance between them, done waiting. They had their lives to gaze upon each other. Right then, she wanted him. All of him. She wrapped her arms around him and drew him back with her to the bed. He didn't need any other encouragement. She was on the bed and beneath him before she could draw in another breath.

She closed her eyes and arched into his touch, the sensations he wrought nearly overwhelming. She'd never dreamed it could be so with a man. Her mother and those of her friends who were married had always described the marriage bed as a chore. Something to be endured. Granted, others had taken a great deal of delight in whatever occurred between a man and a woman. Or so they'd said. Sorcha had never known what to believe.

But now… She gasped again as his lips found her breasts. She had never known such pleasure could exist. Malcolm worshipped her, his hands and lips moving everywhere. He explored every inch of her until he knew her body better than she, until she cried out in pleasure again and again.

He finally settled over her, easing his way inside her with murmured words of love and devotion that she never thought she'd hear from any man, least of all the MacGregor tyrant she'd been forced to wed. How foolish she'd been. Malcolm was everything she'd ever wanted.

The moment of pain was sharp, but quick. Malcolm held steady, stoking her desire with his lips and hands until she moved beneath him again, desperate for more. When he found his own pleasure, she was right there with him. They clung to each other, hearts pounding together, bodies still entwined, until their breathing slowly returned to normal.

Malcolm smoothed the hair from her face and gazed deeply into her eyes. "Are ye all right?"

Sorcha managed a weak laugh. "Better than all right. I never dreamed anything could be quite so…" The blood rushed to her cheeks and she laughed, amazed that after what they'd just done she could still blush.

He laughed with her and leaned down for a tender kiss that quickly turned heated.

"Can we do it again?" she asked.

His chuckle reverberated through her. "Aye, my insatiable wife. Though perhaps no' just yet. Ye may be a bit sore."

He wasn't wrong about that, though the ache wasn't entirely unpleasant. He left her briefly and came back with a pitcher of water and a piece of linen. When he began to clean her she tried to protest but he pushed her hands away. After a moment, her slight embarrassment turned to pleasure, and she moved restlessly.

She hoped his ministrations might turn more amorous, but instead, he wrapped his arms around her and pulled her back against him. She sighed deeply, loving the feel of him wrapped about her. Despite her best intentions, her eyes grew heavy. The third time she jerked herself awake, Malcolm chuckled and kissed the top of her head.

"Let it bide, love. We have our whole lives to explore each other. Rest now. Ye'll need it."

"Will I?"

"Oh, aye. I dinna plan on letting ye out of this bed for at least a week."

That sounded heavenly to her.

Chapter Eighteen

The sound of the warning bell clanging yanked him from near oblivion and sent terror spiking through him. He jumped from the bed and ran to the window. Smoke was visible in the distance in the pale morning light.

"Malcolm, what is it?" Sorcha asked.

He turned to his wife, looking so lovely and innocent with the coverlet pressed modestly to her bosom, her hair mussed about her head.

"Something is burning. One of the villages, perhaps."

"Oh no!"

Malcolm quickly dressed, Sorcha following suit. He hurried about his preparations, though he couldn't keep from watching her. The coincidence of such a raid occurring so soon after Sorcha had sent out a messenger with her father's men still in his courtyard was too much to ignore. He didn't want to believe the obvious. Didn't want to believe the woman he'd just given his heart to could betray him so thoroughly.

She wound her arms around his waist and pressed her cheek to his chest. He did not return her embrace. She glanced up confused but he slowly set her from him just as John burst through the door.

"Malcolm! Raiders. Our outlooks spotted a large squad coming from the east ridge."

"The east?" He looked back at Sorcha. "The side that is still damaged, with no' but a half-built wall to keep them out? How would they ken such a thing about our weakened defenses?"

She may have been confused before, but she wasn't mistaking him now. "How would I know?" She put her hands on her hips, throwing every bit of anger and derision she could at him.

"What have ye done, Sorcha?"

She stared at him, mouth wide with shock. "Nothing. I have done nothing, my lord, I swear it."

"Ye mean me to believe 'tis naught but coincidence that a day after your maid arrives with twenty of your father's men and ye send out a messenger to yer father within an hour of her arrival, that we face an attack at our weakest wall. We've been set up nicely to be attacked from within and without."

"I swear to you, Malcolm, the only message I sent was to tell my father of my happiness and well-being. Nothing more."

One of the page boys ran in, his thin chest heaving as he tried to catch his breath. "My lord, Heatherthorn is burning!"

"Heatherthorn?" Sorcha asked.

John nodded, his face grave. "The small village a few miles from here. They dinna have much of value. The raiders are probably burning their homes out of spite. Or to draw us out."

"Where is your maid, Sorcha?" Malcolm asked.

She looked back to him, startled at the question. "It's barely morning. I'm sure she's in her room, behind my chamber. I haven't seen her since..." Her cheeks blushed hotly but Malcolm couldn't find it in him to pity her. She could have found a moment to slip away, perhaps while he slept. Though, surely he'd have woken. But…there must have been other moments when she could have betrayed him. For someone certainly had. And who had more cause than the daughter of his greatest enemy who'd been forced to wed him? The thought made his chest feel as though it were cleaving in two.

He jerked his head at John who immediately turned to investigate. He returned a few moments later and shook his head and Malcolm looked down at Sorcha with a stony glare.

"Where is she?"

Sorcha shook her head, her face pale and drawn. "I don't know. She was there. I left her there."

"Malcolm, we must go," John said, looking back and forth between Malcolm and his wife as they stared intensely at each other.

Finally, Malcolm nodded his head, a curious numbness spreading through him. *How could I have been so wrong?* And now his people would pay the price.

"Round up the Campbell men who arrived with the baggage wagon. We'll need to split our forces. Send help to Heatherthorn and leave the rest to guard the castle. And just pray it is enough."

John nodded and ran out. Malcolm looked back at his wife. "Ye will stay in these rooms until I return."

"Malcolm, please. You know me. You know I wouldn't do this."

Did I? I thought so.

The tears filling her eyes tore at him. He didn't know what to believe. He wavered.

"My lord!" one of his men shouted. "They are at the wall!"

"Enough," he said. Whether he wanted to believe it or not wouldn't change the facts. And he didn't have time to deal with it just then.

Sorcha opened her mouth to protest but he turned away. He couldn't listen to her lies anymore. His people needed him. He gestured to one of the men in the hall. "Lock this door. Dinna let anyone in or out."

"But, my lord, what if the castle is attacked?"

Malcolm glanced back at her, pain and disappointment crashing through him. "It will be. But if they make it inside, do what ye can to protect the women and children gathered in the hall. Dinna worry about her," he said, unable to bring himself to look at Sorcha again. "They'll no' hurt her. She's one of them."

Sorcha reeled back as if she'd been struck, and for a moment Malcolm wavered. He could still feel her in his arms, her heart beating in time with his own. The memory of her gentle softness pressed against him, her deep blue eyes gazing into his as they made love, would stay with him until his dying day, as would their murmured words of love. Each one now struck him like a knife. Mocked him. Wrecked him.

How could she have said such things, done such things, and not meant them? Surely, she couldn't be so duplicitous.

"We've found the maid, my lord." One of his men dragged a disheveled Berta forward. She yanked her arm from his grasp and stomped over to Sorcha. Sorcha watched her, such a mix of emotions rolling across her face Malcolm couldn't identify them all.

"What have you done, Berta?" she asked.

Berta squared her shoulders and raised her head defiantly, but Malcolm had no desire to her hear lies. "Lock them both in. I'll deal with them when I return."

He marched out with John, ignoring the sound of Sorcha crying out his name, though it pierced him straight through the heart.

He had a battle to prepare for. And for the first time, he wasn't sure it was a battle from which he wanted to return.

Coming home would only mean pain.

• • •

Sorcha rounded on her maid but the woman, for the first time in her life, wouldn't meet her eyes.

"Berta, please tell me you did not do what they are accusing you of."

"I was only trying to help you, my lady."

Sorcha's heart sank to her toes. "By doing what?"

"I didn't think you were safe here, my lady! You are living in the midst of your worst enemies. So when we came upon a group of Campbell men on our journey here and they offered to accompany us…"

"Wait a moment. The men you came here with weren't in your retinue?"

Berta shook her head. "Only four of them. And we all thought it prudent to bring larger numbers."

"Why didn't my father send more men in the first place?"

"He said four would be sufficient to guard the wagon without being so large a force as to offend Lord Glenlyon."

Sorcha paced in front of the fireplace. "He was right. Bringing in a troop of twenty men for one small wagon is almost as good as a declaration of war."

"I understand that now, my lady. And when I saw how you were acting with Lord Glenlyon, I knew we'd made a mistake. It's why I left to try and find the commander of the men who came with us."

"What are you talking about?" Sorcha asked, frowning. "How were we acting?"

"You and he…acting as though…as though you love each other."

Sorcha sank to the chair near her. "As though we loved each other?"

"Yes, my lady." Berta sat on the stool at her feet and reached over to take her hands. "I cannot speak for certain about how Lord Glenlyon feels. Though I can tell you he looked like a man who had never seen the sun but was finally able to feel its warm rays on his face."

Sorcha's eyes widened, hope blossoming in her chest.

"But you, my lady, I have known since you were no more than a babe toddling at my feet. Never have I seen you so taken with a man. As though you lived before, but now you truly breathe. You fairly glow when you are near him. And he around you."

Sorcha released a long breath. "I hadn't dared hope he'd return my feelings. Truth be told, I'm still not exactly sure what my feelings are."

Berta patted her hands. "Your heart knows. Your head will follow in time."

Sorcha snorted. "I don't know. My head can be awfully stubborn."

"And that's the honest truth, my lady."

Men shouted in the courtyard, and Sorcha jumped up and ran to the window. She couldn't make out much from the angle she was at. But the sound of swords clanging together and the battle cries of her new kinsmen made her blood run cold.

Sorcha spun around, her heart thundering in her chest. "I need to get out of here. If those men are here under some misguided crusade to free me from my prison, they need to be told I need no such rescue."

"Forgive me, my lady, but I'm not sure that matters much."

"What do you mean?"

"They used that as the excuse to join our retinue, but I heard them talking when they thought I was asleep. They've been looking for a way past Glenlyon's defenses for months. Joining our group gave them access to the inner walls."

"Why did you go along with this?"

"I told you, my lady, I thought you needed our help. You

were so fearful of coming here you nearly poisoned the man."

Sorcha threw her hands up. "That was an accident! Will I never live that down?"

"Accident or no, that was your frame of mind when you left, and no one has heard from you since. I wasn't even sure I'd find you here at all, let alone knowing in what state. I thought I was doing what was best for you. Ensuring we had enough men from our own clan to give you aid should you need it."

"And if I didn't? You felt no qualms in inviting twenty armed men into a lion's den? Surely you realized there could be a battle."

Berta looked down, shaking her head. "My lady, in all the possible circumstances I envisioned finding you, not once did it occur to me I'd find you happy and in love."

Sorcha snorted at that. "That makes two of us. However, it seems that is what I am. And I'd like to stay that way, so we need to put a stop to this."

"I tried to speak to the commander, to explain. But he wouldn't listen to me."

"Well, he'll listen to me or he'll have my father to answer to."

"That's just it, my lady. These men don't acknowledge your father as their chief. When I mentioned that very thing, they laughed and said…forgive me, my lady, but they said that the old badger wasn't as cunning as he once was and that they would do what they wanted, regardless of his wishes."

Sorcha swore under her breath and went to the door, banging on it until her fist throbbed. The guard Malcolm had stationed outside finally opened the door.

"I'm sorry, milady, but Lord Glenlyon said—"

"I know what he said, but it's imperative I get out of here now."

"But my lady…"

A crash sounded from below, so loud it was as if a cannon had gone off, splintering the front doors. Sorcha's heart leapt to her throat as she realized that could very well be what happened. Screams echoed up the grand staircase.

"Go!" she yelled at the guard. "They need help!"

He didn't wait for her to say it again. Sorcha and Berta followed close on his heels. She skidded to a stop at the top of the stairwell, trying to take in the chaos that reigned below. There were many more than the group of Campbell men that had come with Berta. The MacGregors would have outnumbered them if half their forces hadn't been sent to Heatherthorn. Sorcha's stomach rolled with the knowledge that it must have been a diversion. Malcolm, John, and their men had walked straight into a trap.

"There they are," Sorcha said to Berta, pointing to a group of women and children huddling near the long table at the far end of the hall.

She ran along the gallery that ringed the great hall, dodging bits of debris that flew at them from the fighting below.

"My lady!"

Sorcha glanced along the opposite gallery and saw Mary rushing toward her. They met at the corner.

"We need to get them out of there," Sorcha said, gazing down at the frightened group below their feet.

"There is a passage behind the dais. It leads to the woods behind the north wall."

Sorcha looked at her in surprise, and Mary gave her a frazzled smile. "My kin have worked for the lairds and lived in the castle for as long as I can remember."

"Is there a way down other than the stairs?" Sorcha looked at the staircase where a main bulk of the fighting was happening. There was no getting down that way.

"Aye, mum. If ye're not afraid to climb."

Sorcha raised a brow and Mary led her and Berta to the back corner of the gallery and lifted a trap door. It was a long drop.

"There used to be a rope ladder in the rafters on a hook right here but…" Mary looked again in vain. "It must have been removed for some reason."

"When we were decorating for the feast day, most likely," Sorcha said, looking around for anything else that might be useful. She indicated one of the banners that had been strung up along the rafters.

"That should be sturdy enough to slide down." *Or at least slow our fall.* But she didn't say that part out loud.

They worked to pull the banner down and find something strong enough to tie it to that would support their weight going down. They finally settled on the railing of the banister ringing the gallery. It would have to stretch to the trapdoor which would leave the banner a bit shorter than Sorcha would have liked, but they could jump the last few feet. They didn't have many choices.

The fighting had begun to trickle up the stairs and something had been set on fire. Smoke slowly filled the great hall.

Sorcha leaned over the banister to see what was burning. The tapestry she'd been working on with the village women was up in flames. Fury rushed through her at the wanton destruction of something she'd worked so hard on. Something they'd all worked on together.

"You!" She peered down the hole at the group of women and children below her. Sorcha gestured to one of the serving women who looked as though she had command of the group. The others huddled together the best they could while she stood guarding them.

"Get that tapestry down and into the hearth before the fire spreads," Sorcha ordered.

The woman stared at her gape-mouthed.

"Quickly!" Sorcha ordered.

She snapped her jaw shut, gave Sorcha a sharp nod, and hurried off to do her lady's bidding.

Mary finally got the banner tied off.

"You first," Sorcha said. She held up a hand to ward off her protest. "You know where the secret door is. Start getting them out!"

Mary nodded, grabbed a hold of the banner and slid deftly to the ground.

Sorcha looked at Berta with wide, surprised eyes. "That didn't look so hard."

Berta looked as though she very much disagreed.

"Come on, you next."

"Oh my lady, I can't possibly."

"Yes. You can possibly. And if you don't, you'll be trapped up here with them."

She pointed over at the men who were slowly fighting their way along both sides of the gallery. Every now and then one would fall, or get pushed over the banister to fall on the flagstones below.

Berta raised terrified eyes to Sorcha, who pulled her in for a quick hug. "You can do this. I'll be right behind you."

Berta nodded, hugged the banner to her so tightly her knuckles turned white, and then slowly disappeared as she shimmied through the hole of the trapdoor on her belly, down to the hall below.

Sorcha waited until her maid had reached the bottom safely before taking the banner in hand herself. Another crash sounded from the entrance to the hall as Sorcha reached the halfway point and she stopped her slide long enough to see Malcolm and his men rushing in to join the fight.

Relief to see him crashed over her at the same time that a rush of terror flooded through her—for him. If she'd needed any other confirmation about how she truly felt, she didn't any longer. She loved him. Her body still carried the memory of his touch. As her heart always would. No matter what happened now, she was his, body and soul. And this was her home.

Another crash sounded and she cringed, wondering what had been destroyed, praying no one had been hurt. How could she stop this? She didn't recognize one of the invading men. They certainly wouldn't pay any attention to her if she told them to stop what they were doing, to return to her father. If, in truth, he'd been the one to send them. To go against the Clan Chief was...well, had never been done. At least not in Sorcha's memory. But these men didn't follow her father, if what Berta said was the truth. So what did that mean—that neither her clan by birth or clan by marriage was to blame for the war in which they were embroiled? Then who was?

Malcolm shouted and led his men into the fray. Sorcha covered her mouth with her hands to keep from screaming his name. Doing so would only distract him. The only thing she could do now was pray. Pray that he'd make it through this alive, so she could knock some sense into his stubborn head. And her father's. All these years of raids and skirmishes and she didn't think the men had ever sat together long enough to compare notes and discover who was really behind all the trouble. They'd never been able to without trying to kill each other. But perhaps, with her help, they would listen to each other now.

As long as Malcolm could stay alive long enough. Until then...she had to do something. Before they destroyed her home. And all those she'd come to love.

Her head swam and renewed her grip on the banner. She watched as Malcolm's eyes scanned the room, until they locked onto hers with wide astonishment. He couldn't stare for long though. Her father's forces immediately swarmed

him, and he began to slash his way through them, obviously
making his way to her. To kill her or protect her, she wasn't
sure.

She quickly slid the rest of the way down and helped the
last few of the women and children out the secret door. Sorcha
looked around but didn't see anyone else they could send out.
She was about to follow herself when a maid Sorcha had seen
working in the kitchens ran to her, a Campbell soldier bearing
down on her. The girl dove into Sorcha's arms, and she spun,
shoving her toward the hidden door.

Berta lurched out of the way so the maid could race past
her, but the girl didn't get far. The Campbell man shoved
Sorcha out of the way, and lunged for the girl. Berta shrieked
and grabbed a chair near the door. Swinging it high, she
brought it down on his head, just as he caught the flying skirts
of the servant girl. The skirts tore in his hand, and the man
dropped to the floor and didn't move.

Sorcha's eyes widened in surprise. Berta wiped her hands
off on her skirts and kicked at the fallen man with a muttered
curse. More men rushed toward where they stood. Sorcha
would never reach the door before they did. The fallen man
and too much debris stood in her way.

"Berta, go! Now!"

Berta squared her shoulders and stepped back into the
hall, slamming the hidden door shut behind her. "Not without
you, my lady!"

She took up a piece of the broken chair and began
to swing it at any man who ventured too close, preventing
anyone from getting to the door.

Sorcha grabbed a torch off the wall to join in, but before
she could move, a shout drew her attention.

She turned just as another Campbell man reached her, his
sword raised to strike.

"Ah!" Malcolm charged him, his sword clanging off his

opponent's as he attacked. "Sorcha! Go!" he yelled to her.

He'd decided not to kill her after all. She nearly smiled. He swung his sword at her attacker, slashing through his side and dropping the man to his knees. Malcolm looked up and met her eyes. She took a step toward him.

Then movement from the gallery above him caught her attention—a Campbell man with a bow, an arrow notched and ready to fly.

"No!" she screamed.

She jumped over the man at her feet and threw herself at Malcolm.

He caught her and stumbled back, his mouth wide with surprise. The hiss of the arrow ended in a screaming jolt of pure agony in her back.

She gasped, the excruciating fire fading to a curious numbness spreading through her.

"Sorcha," Malcolm rasped, holding her to him.

Her legs crumpled, and he swept her into his arms.

"Sorcha!"

Her head lolled against his chest.

He was warm. He was safe. Everything would be fine now.

"Malcolm," she whispered. Her voice wouldn't work right. But that didn't matter. Malcolm held her. That was all she needed to know.

The last thing she saw was Malcolm bent over her calling her name, those beautiful amber eyes staring into hers. Her lion, protecting her to the last.

Then the black spots eating at her vision filled the world.

Chapter Nineteen

The aftermath of the battle still lay littered about the hall, along with the injured who had been gathered together near the hearth so they could be cared for. Malcolm sat between two pallets watching the two people he loved the most in the world, making sure their chests continued to rise and fall. Every time they faltered, even for a second, he jumped, his heart ricocheting in his chest.

"You need to get some rest, my lord," Berta said, coming over to check the bandage covering her mistress's chest, then the one at her back. "They are both doing well. But you won't be able to do them any good if you make yourself ill."

"Later," Malcolm said, waving her off. He wasn't leaving their sides.

"My lord…" Berta paused, gnawing at her lower lip. "I wanted to say again how sorry I was that I was misled. That I caused…"

Malcolm shook his head, too heart-sore and worried to deal with the maid's guilt just then. "We'll discuss it later."

"But, my lord…"

He sighed. "It would ha' come sooner or later. Ye made a mistake. One that cost us dear," he said, looking at Sorcha's pale face. "But be that as it may, I dinna think yer purpose was ought but to save yer mistress. And ye fought brawly by her side when it counted. Let it bide."

"Thank you, my lord." Berta sniffed and wiped her nose on her sleeve.

Malcolm still hadn't taken his eyes from his wife. "But…" he said, the words torn from a place deep inside that roiled and screamed in agony, "if she dies…"

Berta blanched. "If she dies, my lord, I'll hand you the dagger to end my life myself."

Malcolm glanced up at her. The pain on her face as she gazed at her mistress was near as great as his own. Aye. If Sorcha died, it wouldn't matter if Malcolm killed her or no. She'd do the deed herself.

"A bit harsh there, aye? She acquitted herself rather well in battle."

Malcolm jerked his head to the other pallet and gazed down at John. "Well, ye wee bastard. Looks like ye'll live after all." He spoke with the same lighthearted tone he and John always used with each other, though the fear he'd felt when he'd watched his cousin fall still coursed through him. The sword wound in his leg was serious, but he shouldn't lose use of the leg. The head wound he'd sustained when falling had concerned Malcolm more. He'd known more than one man who'd never woken after a blow to the head.

John snorted. "Aye, I'll do. Thanks to her," he said, nodding at Berta. "If she hadna clubbed the man whose sword was aimed at the more impressive bits of my anatomy, I wouldna be here to regale ye with tales of my prowess."

Malcolm chuckled. "Oh, aye?" He glanced back at Berta. "Well, I suppose saving the life, or at least the pride, of my kinsman would make her deserving of my pardon."

Berta covered her mouth with her apron, her eyes bright with unshed tears. She gave Malcolm a little curtsy and scurried off for more hot water and bandages.

Malcolm focused on his cousin's pale face. "How are ye, Jack? Truly?"

John's eyebrows rose. "Ye havena called me Jack since we were lads. I must be worse off than I feel, which isna all that grand, to tell the truth. I must be at death's door, surely."

Malcolm chuckled. "If ye're able to spout all that nonsense, ye must be better than ye look."

John's gaze took him in. "And how about you? Ye should listen to her and get some rest," he said, his voice raspy but strong. "Ye look like hell."

Malcolm looked down at his best friend and kinsman and smiled. "Well, coming from you, I'll take that as compliment."

"I would," John said. "Ye're no' so much to look at under normal circumstances."

Malcolm chuckled quietly. John could always make him laugh. Even during the most inappropriate times.

"So what am I doing down here?" John asked, indicating the makeshift bed on which he lay. "Are all my bits still attached?"

Malcolm sobered. "Aye, though it was a near thing for some of them." He nodded down at John's leg and John rose up enough so he could see the bandage that stretched from his groin to his knee. He cursed under his breath.

"Ye're sure I'm all there?"

"You can check, if ye dinna believe me."

John shook his head. "I canna bring myself to look." He lifted the corner of his blanket. "Ye'll have to do it for me."

Malcolm laughed and knocked John's hand off the blanket. "It's no matter anyway, laddie. Ye'll no' be needing it for some time yet, in any case."

John sighed. "Well, that's a cryin' shame. It's a bit like

depriving Michelangelo of his paintbrush."

Malcolm snorted. "Aye, I know ye'll be fine when ye start spouting yer delusions of grandeur."

"No' delusions, if they're the truth." He grinned and lay back down with a grimace he couldn't quite hide. Before Malcolm could ask him how he was again, John nodded at Sorcha.

"How is she?"

All levity dropped from Malcolm at once and he took his wife's limp hand in his own again.

"I dinna ken yet. She's alive. For now."

"That's one brave lass."

"Aye. Stubborn as an ox and half as smart, but brave... aye, I'll gi'ye that."

John chuckled. "Stubborn maybe, but then she'd need to be so, married to you. As for her wits...well, I'll no' say marryin' ye was a mark in her favor, but other than that, she seems a fair bit brighter than either of the two of us."

Malcolm snorted. "I wouldna call throwing herself in front of an arrow a particularly intelligent thing to do."

"She did it to save yer life," John said quietly.

Malcolm nodded and swallowed hard, each word striking him like a red hot brand. "Aye." He closed his other hand over hers, wishing he could wrap his whole body around her and keep her safe. "It wasna worth the price."

"She thought so."

Malcolm glanced briefly at his cousin before returning his gaze to Sorcha's still, pale face. "Aye, well, she'd never admit it, but she's almost never right."

John chuckled quietly, the sound breaking off in a hiss of pain. Malcolm made to stand but John waved him away. "I'll do. Ye tend to her."

Malcolm watched him for a moment to make sure he was truly well and then went back to his silent vigil.

"Ye love her, don't you?" John asked.

Malcolm raised startled eyes to him. "I…" He shook his head. "What I said to her…before… She hates me now."

John rolled his eyes. "If that were true, you would be the one lying there."

"It should be me," Malcolm said fiercely.

"Aye, because ye love her."

Malcolm went back to staring at Sorcha, his thumb slowly stroking her hand. Over and over. "It doesna matter. If she lives, I'm going to give her what she wants. I'll go to the king, tell him I'm petitioning for an annulment. Take all the blame."

"On what grounds?"

"It doesna matter. I'll think of something."

"Are ye certain that's what she still wishes? Lassies ha' been known to change their minds from time to time."

Malcolm snorted. "No' this one. I've never met a more stubborn, bull-headed—"

"That's a fine way to show gratitude."

Malcolm sucked in a startled breath and stopped rambling, looking down in surprise. A pair of dark blue eyes blinked up at him, trying to focus before she sighed and gave up, closing them again.

He leaned over her and kissed her forehead. "Sorcha? Open your eyes again, *mo chridhe*."

"There you go, trying to order me about again. And speaking of hearts, is mine intact?"

"Aye. Barely, but aye, it is." Malcolm chuckled, utter joy pulsing through him so strongly it was all he could do to keep from scooping her up and swinging her around.

"Is there water?" she asked, her voice hoarse.

"Aye."

A glass was pressed into his hand before he could even move to look for one. Berta stood behind them with tears in her eyes and helped him sit Sorcha up enough for her to drink some water. She lay back down with a gasp.

"If I'd known it was going to hurt this bad, I might have let you take it instead."

She said it with a smile, but Malcolm's heart clenched remembering her slumping in his arms, the arrow protruding from her shoulder. It had gone clean through, far enough to pierce his chest. Deep enough to leave a small scar, though not to injure him. It was nothing more than a scratch to him. But her…

He slipped from the stool to sink to his knees beside the pallet and clasped her hand between his, raising it to his forehead as if he were praying. When he thought he could raise his head without unleashing the tears that burned in his throat, he looked at her. She gazed at him, her eyes wide with her own unshed tears.

"Why did ye do it, Sorcha?"

She stared at him for a moment. "It seemed like the thing to do at the time."

He gave her a small smile. "If ye'd let me die, all yer problems would ha' been solved. All very convenient and civilized for ye. Ye could have returned back to court a respectable widow."

"True. But I've gotten rather used to being inconvenienced. I'm sure life as a respectable widow would be rather boring. Besides, returning to court would require another several weeks of travel and I am never making that journey again."

He laughed at that. "I dinna care to repeat it any time soon either, I'll grant ye that." He stared at her for a moment longer. Her eyes blinked slowly, as if she were fighting off sleep. He should let her rest. But he had to know. Needed to know.

"Why, Sorcha?" he asked again, his voice cracking on the last word. "I'm no' worth your life."

"Yes, you are."

His breath left him in a rush, and the lump he'd been fighting in his throat grew even larger.

"Ye hated me, though," he choked out.

"Maybe I've grown accustomed to hating you. Maybe I love to hate you." Her smile slowly grew. "Or maybe I just love you."

He leaned over and gently kissed her. "Maybe I love ye, too." He kissed her again. "But promise me ye'll stop throwing yerself in front of arrows."

She didn't laugh as he'd expected her too. Instead, her brow furrowed. "What of my father? He still sees you as the enemy, still believes you are attacking him without provocation. What happened to his men?"

"We managed to subdue them. Barely." He sat back though he didn't release her hand. "They are currently awaiting the arrival of your father. We sent a messenger to him letting him know what occurred here. Timothy arrived not an hour ago wi' word that your father would come personally to handle this matter."

"Are you sure he won't be arriving with an army?"

"Nay. But I have hope once he gets here and hears the truth of the matter from ye, he will relent."

"My father has never been one to relent easily. However, seeing as how there hasn't been a raid on Campbell lands since our marriage, that I've heard of, in any case, and there have been several against our men, he'll have no choice but to believe."

"Our men?" Malcolm asked, his heart warming at her use of the word *our*.

"Yes, ours. Don't gloat."

"Aye, my lady," he said, kissing her hand.

She smiled at him and weakly squeezed his hand. "Now what?"

"Well." He leaned over her. "You heal. Quickly. One

night with ye wasna nearly enough. We have some lost time to make up for."

She chuckled. "I'll see what I can do."

He captured her lips again, kissing her long and, deep, until his knees began to cramp from kneeling on the stone floor.

Sorcha smiled up at him. "Someday you'll have to explain to me how trying to drive you away won your love."

He laughed at that and kissed her again. "Perhaps I enjoy being miserable."

"*Hmm*, yes, that seems like the type of obstinate thing you'd enjoy."

"Only promise me ye'll never stop."

She entwined her fingers with his. "Now that I can do."

Epilogue

Malcolm paced the sitting room, anxiety roiling through him until he was like to explode. John sat watching, an expression somewhere between amusement and concern etched on his face. Malcolm's fist clenched. If his cousin smiled, he'd be picking up a few teeth from the floor.

"Sit down, Malcolm. Drink." He pushed another tumbler full of whisky his way.

Sitting wasn't an option, but drinking he could do. He reached for the glass but froze as another scream echoed through the closed bedchamber door and ripped through his soul.

"Enough!" Malcolm said, stalking to the door. "There must be something wrong. I'll not stand here while Sorcha's ripped apart and do nothing about it."

John stood and tried to stop him but Malcolm wasn't having it. His wife needed him, and he was damn well going to go to her.

Before he could open the door, Mrs. Bryd poked her head out. "What's all this ruckus out here?" She didn't give him a chance to answer but looked over at John. "I told ye to take him away from the keep. We've work to do in here and listening to him roaring and blustering about is distracting my lady. Shoo," she said to Malcolm.

"But she screamed—"

"O' course she did," Mrs. Bryd said, looking at him like he'd lost his mind. He certainly felt like he had. "She's trying to birth yer child, ye great dithering fool. It's hard work." Her face softened a bit as she looked at him, and she came out of the chamber far enough to pat his arm. "My lady is strong and healthy and is doing verra well, I promise ye. It shouldn't be long now. Go with John. There's naught ye can do here. Yer part was done months ago."

She went back in the room, chuckling at her ribald jest.

John clapped a hand on Malcolm's shoulder and led him from the room in a bit of a daze. He'd caught a glimpse of Sorcha's pale, straining face over Mrs. Bryd's shoulder. Leaving her to labor alone went against every instinct he had.

He stopped short before John could lead him outdoors. "Nay," he said. "I'll not go so far. She may have need of me."

Fortunately, John didn't try to force him but waved instead to a seat before the large hearth in the main hall. Malcolm's body was tense, ready to spring. He felt as though a battle were imminent and he must be ready. The truth, he supposed. A battle was indeed being waged, only it wasn't his to fight. A fact that made him want to tear his hair out by the roots.

"Malcolm, do ye mind what I told ye last night?"

"Hmm?" Malcolm said, too distracted to focus clearly on John.

"I'll stay for the child's christening, but then I must go," John said.

That got Malcolm's attention. "What d'ye mean?"

"We've discussed this before, Cousin. I must finish what I started when I was at court last. I canna stand by anymore while those who profited during Cromwell's reign go free. We saw more abuses at court when last we were there. And while ye've been here enjoying yer newfound happiness, as ye should," he said, holding out his hand to stop Malcolm's protest, "I've been doing a fair bit of thinking."

"A dangerous thing to do, or so Sorcha tells me," Malcolm said with a smile.

"Aye, that 'tis. But I canna sit by any longer. I must do something or go mad. Besides, I have estates of my own that I've sore neglected these past years."

"True enough."

John sighed and ran a hand through his hair. "Charles canna do much about it. He has to appease too many factions. And those like that bastard Lord Harding have gone too long without answering for their crimes."

"And you plan to do something about that, eh?"

John gave him a crooked smile. "Aye, maybe a bit."

Malcolm reached over and clasped his shoulder. "Just don't stay away too long, ye hear? I know ye have yer own holdings, but Glenlyon is yer home and ye'll always belong here by my side."

"Thank ye, Cousin. I'll no' stay away too long."

"My lord."

Malcolm and John looked up to see Berta standing there, her usually dour face beaming. "My lady wishes a word with you, my lord."

Malcolm was up and taking the stairs two at a time before Berta had finished speaking. He burst into Sorcha's bedchamber, stopping short at the incredible sight of his beautiful wife cradling a tiny bundle.

• • •

Sorcha looked up when Malcolm rushed into the room, hair

flying and eyes wild. She smiled up at him, pure joy dancing through her heart. "*Mo leòmhann.* Come and meet your son."

The awe and wonder that shone from Malcolm's face as he took his sleeping son in his arms was almost more than Sorcha could bear. How could one heart hold so much love and happiness without bursting at the seams? She lay back against the pillows and basked in the sight of her husband cradling their tiny babe.

Malcolm leaned over and kissed her tenderly. "How do ye fare, *mo chridhe*?"

"Better than you, I think," she said with a chuckle that stopped short on a hiss of pain. Malcolm's brow furrowed but she waved him away. "I am perfectly all right, I promise. Just a bit tired. And sore. Your son is every bit the brawny warrior already."

"Aye," Malcolm said, the awe back in his voice as he gazed down at their child slumbering in his arms. "That he is." He drew a finger across the child's face. "He needs a name."

"I thought, perhaps, John," she said, smiling gently when Malcolm's startled gaze met hers.

"John. Aye. 'Tis a good name for a strapping wee laddie."

"And William, for your father and brother."

Malcolm's eyes were suspiciously bright when he nodded his head. "Ye honor me, my wife."

"Our boy should be named for fine, strong men. I can think of no better than naming him for the men who are responsible for you. And naming him for his grandfather is tradition, after all."

He smiled at her, amber eyes bright with emotion. "I have a suggestion of my own."

Sorcha waited, curious as a small smile played along Malcolm's lips.

"Angus."

She sucked in a breath, more surprised than if he'd suddenly decided to name their child after Berta. "You wish to name him for my father?"

"Well, he did produce you. So there must be some redeeming qualities to the man."

She laughed again, carefully, and reached over to caress his cheek. "You'll never cease to amaze me."

"Besides, we owe the man a debt. Discovering his own son, your half-brother, had been behind the raids on our clan couldn't have been pleasant. Would have been easy to turn a blind eye, or perhaps ship the boy off to the continent. Not turn him over to the king for justice as he did."

Sorcha frowned at that. She had never been close to her half-brother, Fergus. In fact, she'd only met him on a very few occasions. "Will his punishment be harsh, do you think?"

"Nay, not nearly what he deserves, I'm sure. Yer father showed a great deal of integrity bringing his own son to justice, I'll grant him that. But I doubt he'd have done so if the punishment would have been more than he was willing to give."

"Then we may not have seen the last of him."

Malcolm sighed and brushed her hair back from her face with his free hand. "I dinna ken for sure. But I dinna believe so, no." He leaned forward to kiss her forehead. "Pay him no mind now. He's safe away for the time being."

The babe let out a little squawk, and Malcolm glanced down in surprise. "Aye, laddie, bide yer time. Yer mam is right here."

He gave her the baby and sat beside her on the bed, wrapping them both in his arms. He leaned down and kissed her, slow and deep. Oh, how she loved this fierce, passionate man!

"Thank you, *mo chridhe*, for my son. I love ye, more than ye'll ever know."

"I love you too, *mo leòmhann*. Never leave my side."

"Never," he agreed, kissing her again.

Another protest from their son had them both laughing.

"John William Angus Campbell MacGregor," Malcolm said, placing a kiss on his son's brow. "Welcome to the world, laddie."

Acknowledgments

A huge thanks to my amazing editor, Erin Molta, who started my new love affair with the MacGregor lairds with her encouragement to explore the wonderful world of Highlanders. I don't think I've ever fallen in love with a book I've written quite so much. Thank you so much for everything! Heads up though, I don't think I'll ever get over my "just" habit. I try, I swear! I *just* can't seem to help myself! Thanks also to Alethea Spiridon, whose enthusiasm gave me the boost I really needed to get through the homestretch. I am so blessed to be able to work with such incredible editors, and all the other fabulous people at Entangled Publishing, without whom my books would still be sitting collecting dust somewhere. To Sarah Ballance, my lovely #creepytwin— it would be a dark, dreary world without you. Also, I don't remember where we left off over on Kira's pages, but I believe it had something to do with spiders and jalapenos, both of which I am still vehemently against. Add mice and their couch-raiding tendencies to my list. Apparently Alejandro decided to move in. I am not amused. And to my sweet family,

I feel like I can do anything with you in my corner. Thank you for putting up with me, for pitching in around the house, and for only mildly complaining when I try to trick you into thinking it's your bedtime an hour early because it's so dark outside. My sweet hubs, thank you for taking all my car pool shifts, and pretending you like it when I cook. I promise I'll think about getting a dog. Maybe. We'll see.

About the Author

Michelle is a jeans and T-shirt kind of girl who secretly wishes she could run around town in a big, poofy dress from the 1600s and hopes to someday be able to get away with crazy stuff like that by chalking it up to her eccentric writer personality. She's addicted to chocolate and goldfish crackers and occasionally writes by hand just so she can hear the scratchy sound of her favorite gel pen on a sheet of paper. She has a B.S. in History, an M.A. in English, and spent most of her formative years with her nose in a book. She loves history and romance and enjoys spending her time combining the two in her novels. She also writes contemporary romance as Kira Archer.

When Michelle's not editing, reading, or chasing her kids around, she can usually be found in a quiet corner working on her next book. She resides in PA with her husband, two children, and three very spoiled cats.

Get Scandalous with these historical reads...

THE ROGUE OF ISLAY ISLE
a *Highland Isles* novel by Heather McCollum

Cullen Duffie is the new chief of Clan MacDonald. Determined to prove he's not his father, Cullen works to secure his clan against the English. When a woman washes onto Islay's shores, he protects her from his uncles' schemes. Waking up not knowing who she is or where she comes from, Madeleine is at the mercy of the man who found her. Through dreams and flashes of her past, she rebuilds her memories. But the more she recalls, the more she realizes the jeopardy she is bringing to Islay, Clan MacDonald, and the Highlander who has captured her heart.

UNMASKING THE EARL
a *Wayward in Wessex* novel by Elizabeth Keysian

The Earl of Stranraer is out for revenge. But his enemy has an unlikely protector—an innocent but headstrong miss who's determined to learn the art of seduction...any way she can. Stranraer does his best to protect her from the notorious rake he's bent on destroying, but in the process the earl gets an unexpected lesson of his own—in forgiveness...and love.

TEMPTING THE PIRATE
a *Love on the High Seas* novel by Tamara Hughes

Charity Goswick thinks she is escaping an arranged marriage to a brute when she slips onto a ship unnoticed. Little does she realize that it's a pirate ship. Now she has been locked in the cabin of a handsome rake of a pirate who sparks the most unladylike feelings within her. But as violence and danger mount on the high seas, Charity will have to put all of her trust in the most untrustworthy of men...a pirate.

Made in the USA
Coppell, TX
29 January 2024